T0209962

NATURAL SELECTION

A NOVEL BY

FREDERICK BARTHELME

COUNTERPOINT

Library of Congress Cataloging-in-Publication Data
Barthelme, Frederick, 1943-
Natural selection : a novel / by Frederick Barthelme. —1ˢᵗ
Counterpoint pbk. ed.

p. cm.

ISBN 1-58243-131-0 (pbk. : alk. Paper)
1. Runaway husbands—Fiction. 2. Fathers and sons—Fiction. 3.
Midlife crisis—Fiction. 4. Houston (Tex.)—Fiction. I. Title.
PS3552.A763 N3 2001
813' .54—dc21
2001028843

COUNTERPOINT
2560 Ninth Street Suite 318
Berkeley, CA 94710

ISBN: 978-1-58243-131-4

Printed in the United States of America

For my mother and father

NATURAL SELECTION

1 I promised Lily I was going to quit complaining
about things, about my job, about the people I
worked with, about the way things were at home
with her, about our son Charles and the way he sometimes
didn't seem to be coming along, about the country, about
Nightline and *Crossfire,* about the mess we live in, the mess
we make of our lives every day, about everybody lying all
the time, smug and self-satisfied and just close enough to
the facts to get by. "It's a disease that's taken over the country," I said. "Just look around, anywhere, any direction,
somebody's lying."

"Yo, Peter," Lily said. "They did a show on it already."

"Yeah, the shiny-hair guy. I saw it."

She patted my arm. "I wonder if we could try to dis-
cipline ourselves a bit? These aren't great complaints, you
know. They're tired, and small, and self-serving, they're
vague—if I weren't wife-of-wives I'm not certain I'd be
charmed."

"Sure you would," I said.

Lily and I were out on the deck in back of our house.

We had a house southwest of Houston in a subdivision called Lazy Lakes, though there weren't any lakes. The development had a few trees, it was quiet, most of the neighbors minded their own business, property values were up some. The house was painfully ordinary, the architecture mundane, the materials cheap, unremarkable, the interior routine, all of that on a site that was a duplicate of a thousand others, a place without any possible interest. But then time passed, and even the most inept house, left standing, allowed to weather, eventually seems to take on the shine of a place that's seen some things. The trees start looking like trees, the yard has worn patches you recognize, the fence is broken in known ways and known places, the cheap Mexican brick suddenly looks like lovely stone. And the deck looks as old as you are; you don't mind sitting on it.

Lily was on the railing. I was standing beside her, looking at the yard, petting the cat. That afternoon we'd found the cat eating a squirrel, from the head down. I dug a hole for the remaining half-a-squirrel, shoveled it in.

Lily said, "That happens every time we feed her chicken-and-beef feast, you know? I figured it out."

"That's crazy," I said, skirting the cat's jaw.

"Are you really going to quit? Complaining?"

"It's my enduring ambition," I said.

Son Charles, who was almost ten, was in the yard arguing about the hose with a neighbor, a little girl named Christine, who was younger and belonged to this guy who lived next door. She was there for dinner.

"Where's Bud tonight?" I said.

"Concert or something. Big date."

"Bud Patrick has a big date?"

Charles had the nozzle tweaked up to maximum thrust,

and he was spattering water all around Christine, making her dance to get out of the way.

"Charles," I said, waving at him to tell him to get the hose away from Christine. "Quit screwing around, O.K.?"

"Ah, Dad. I'm not hurting her. I'm just playing with her. We're just playing."

"We are not," Christine said. "I'm not, anyway. I don't know what he's doing." She twisted herself into crossed limbs, a posture that spoke in big letters.

"Do the bushes," Lily said to Charles. "They need water."

"At work a guy'll come in and make a big argument for his promotion and when he's done I don't even know what world he's talking about. Remember the intern we had last fall, kid from Colorado? We hired him because he made friends with Lumming and what's-his-name, the guy in production—Mossy? Isn't that it? Something. So the personnel group met and Lumming and Mossy said the kid was the greatest. What they didn't say was he's good at dinner parties, the wives like him. So we hired the kid because he's charming at table, only nobody ever said that. We should burn all three of them, no question."

She rolled the Weber barbecue kettle into place, tapped her foot, eyed me.

"We cooking out tonight?" I said.

"You," she said. "It's a new therapy, very big in the Southwest. Homegrown. We're tired of waiting on California. My brother Ray, who has spent time in California as you know, tells me we no longer have to wait."

Ray was the bad brother, given to jumbo concepts and get-garish-quick schemes untainted by the reek of success; I liked him. "How's Ray doing?" I said.

"Ray's on the comeback," she said. "He called and said he even has a job lined up."

"That'll be new. I'm not sure I know how to act in a world in which Ray goes to work in the morning."

"I'm not sure you know how to act period," Lily said. She tapped her foot more, larger taps this time. "You ready?"

I was glad she was running this. I watched her mess with the barbecue, setting it up, wiggling old ashes out, scraping the grill. I wondered if I used to be more easygoing, if that wasn't what I missed most.

"What am I cooking?" I asked.

"Lamb chops," she said.

This made me feel better. Lamb chops and suddenly the world was new, a place of mystery and possibility. Lily and my mother were the only women on the planet who still *believed* in lamb chops.

She was redistributing the coals in the kettle, leveling them. Then she squatted beside the cooker and wiggled the bottom vent back and forth again, releasing the last ashes into the catcher, which she dumped over the side of the deck. Then she said, "I am thinking limas and corn, vegetably speaking."

I went into the storage closet that opened onto the deck, looking for barbecue tools. In there, poking around, I had this momentary idea that other people, at the office, in the neighborhood, were doing better. They were deeply in love, deeply contented, committed to each other, ready to ignore the odd truant passion, bound to their spouses, eager to get home night after night to the familiar pockets of fat and red creases where legs met buttocks, to see the new slack-look breasts, the wrinkled nipples, the bulging stomachs and hair-thick backs, the absent chins. They keenly yearned to hear the partner's stories of daily conquest, or the wan recollections, or the dearly held and only incidentally forlorn wishes. How did they do this, I wondered.

None of it fit Lily, anyway. Lily was lovely. That we only made love now and then, and that when we did I was going through motions and assumed she was, too, worried me, but I wasn't desperate. I didn't loathe it. And I liked the accidental, more casual stuff that happened without thought, the friendly intimacy we had.

What brought this to mind, I thought as I arranged my cooking gear—barbecue tongs, mesquite chips, lighter fluid—on the redwood table, was a TV show I had seen the night before on CNN. On the show a Los Angeles sex therapist answered all our questions. She was on at midnight, when all our sex questions usually slink to mind. What struck me was that this woman made a lot of assumptions about the rest of us, about her viewers and her callers. About me. She managed, without actually saying it, to root her answers to our earnest questions in an adolescent ideal, the model every drive-in psychologist, television evangelist, and frill-inclined spouse seems to cling to—a man and a woman expressing deep emotions in happy copulation together forever. I don't know where this idea came from, and I certainly don't know what its subscribers say to each other before, during, or after their congress, or what they think when one or the other is at the shopping mall dying to fuck the face off some teenager in a ripped-open shirt and wonderfully bad jeans—maybe they just rush home and say their prayers, beg forgiveness for the sin, the sin that almost was and the sin of getting close to the sin that almost was. Maybe they confess, do penance, seek absolution. Maybe they get it.

This woman therapist on TV took callers' questions, acted openly sympathetic, smiled and nodded her attractive head in deep and genuine and marketable compassion, and then answered with the dull-witted assurance that characterizes and haunts us these days—this is the way it should be, it's O.K. the way it is, here are the solutions to your problems, follow these three easy steps, put your little foot, put your little foot, put your little foot right here.

I got angry watching this program. Somebody called from Fairfax, Virginia, and said sex wasn't interesting anymore and didn't this hotshot West Coast therapist know that, even? She wanted to know why this woman on TV didn't get real.

That made me feel better. I watched for an hour. The woman wore a lot of makeup. Not as much as Cleopatra, but plenty, more than enough. She was good-looking, a dark-skin dark-hair type, with prime eyes and a handful of lovely freckles, but there was the unmistakable shadow of the born-again about her, there was that earnestness that makes you want to shoot first and ask questions later, or just shoot and forget the questions. Everybody's born-again these days; if you're not born-again you're dead, you're out of touch, yours is a minority view, you lose. Cash it in, Fuckface. This woman had a convenient rapport with the announcer, who was a newsman, and they traded asides and micro-jokes between callers' questions. The newsguy apologized a lot about his hopeless manhood. "Hey, it happens, right?" he finally said, shrugging into the camera. "We'll be right back."

. . .

When I got to doing the barbecue I didn't make too much of a mess, though I was hacked when I brought in the chops and dribbled lamb juice on the carpet in the living room. This was nine-dollar-a-yard carpet, nothing to get ardent about, but I didn't want blood dots all over it, either. Before

I had time to get worse Lily had the plate of chops out of my hands and was telling me to remember three weeks before when I threw barbecue at the kitchen window.

"That was pork," I said. "Medallions of pork. That's all I ever throw. It's a thing with me. And I don't know why you feel you have to remind me about it all the time, anyway. I cleaned it up, didn't I?"

"Yes, Peter," she said. She was circling the table, slapping lamb chops on the plates. "It took you two hours."

"But it was real cool, Dad," Charles said, making a throwing move. "Splat!"

I said, "No, my little Dustbuster, it was not cool."

"You threw the food?" Christine said. "That sounds funny. Why did you do that?"

"How old is she?" I asked Lily. I kissed the top of Christine's head and then took my chair. "If you're real good," I said to Christine, "we can get you a dog later, O.K.? To take home."

"Peter," Lily said, catching me with a look that meant I was headed for a bad zone.

"You're trying too hard again, Dad," Charles said. He had taken to adding "Dad" to every sentence. It was annoying. Besides, he was way ahead of me on the dog thing.

"Yeah, Dad," Lily said. "Take it easy, would you?" She pinched Charles's ear and turned him to face his dinner.

Charles squirmed, trying to get away from her. "Jesus, Mom," he said.

"None of that, kid," I said. I waved my fork at him for emphasis, pointed it at him, wiggled it in his face like I was scrambling a couple of eggs.

"You're not really getting me a dog," Christine said. "Who wants a stupid dog, anyway?" She was using an overhand grip on her spoon, shoving the food on her plate around to make sure that nothing touched anything else. Once Lily had tried to help her, but the next day her mother called and explained that she'd been doing it since she was four, that Christine would grow out of it. Lily had said she wished somebody would teach the woman a parenting skill, just one.

"Charles wants a dog," I explained to the girl. "You remember Charles?" I pointed at him again, again with the fork. "All he's said for the last three weeks is how much he wants a dog."

"That was before," Charles said. "I don't want a dog now."

"Oh yeah? Before what?" Christine said. She turned to me as if we were co-conspirators. "He wants one, Mr. Wexler. I know he does. He's a liar, he's lying."

"We don't say that over here," Lily said. "Peter?"

"I'm afraid she's right, Christine. Don't call Charles a liar, O.K.? It's not nice. I wish it was O.K. but it's not. I don't make the laws around here, I just enforce them. Are you with me on this one?" I was finished with lamb chop number one. The mint-flavored apple jelly was glistening on my plate. It looked like a miniature, angular stoplight. I felt better. I looked at Charles and wondered if he was O.K. on the dog joke. I hoped.

"I'll bet it's true, though," Christine said. She was playing with her food. Twirling her chop in the clear space she'd left for it on her plate.

"I used to want a dog," Charles said, "but now I don't. Can't anybody understand that? What's the big deal? Dogs can't even talk."

"I understand it," Christine said.

"Eat your dinner," Lily said. "Both of you. You can understand it later, O.K.?"

"Aww, Mom," Charles said, poking at his lima beans. "Eat," I said.

I knew I shouldn't do the dog stuff, tell him we were when we weren't, but he knew we weren't, and why: Dad was bad about dogs. Dad looked at a dog and saw a travel club for ticks and fleas. Try explaining that to a kid—*It's a flea, see? Jumps around. Bites. Multiplies ravenously. Charles?*

Lily and I had big fights about the dog, but I outlasted her. I wasn't proud of it, but it was O.K. I didn't mind winning one every now and then. She still thought I'd come around, but she was wrong. When I was a kid I liked dogs— I had a couple, strays, one called George, one called Poochy. I had rabbits, too. Even fish. I told Charles he could have fish, but he didn't want fish. I said fish were great and he said, "Prove it."

So there was a history about this dog stuff, in the family; I teased Charles and Lily—maybe it was cruel, but it seemed to me they ought to understand. You can't always get what you want and all that. Once no dog was looming on the horizon casting the big shaggy shadow, then the subject was fair game. Lily said I was crazy, kids don't operate the way we do. She said I was building distrust. She said it wasn't smart, that when I was old Charles would trick me—tell me he was coming to see me and then not show, or take me out for a drive and slam me into an old people's home.

"O.K.," I said, restarting the subject at the dinner table. "I'm sorry I brought up the dog. The dog remark was a bad idea. No dog. I wish I could find room in my heart for a dog but I can't. Charles?"

"What?" He was standoffish and cool, much older than his years. 'I know," he said.

"I shouldn't have said a thing about the dog, O.K.? I don't know why I did. I'm upset."

"Dad's upset about the office, sweetheart," Lily said.

"He shouldn't take it out on me," Charles said. He turned, gave me a real adult look. "You shouldn't, Dad."

I didn't think I liked the way Charles was turning out. For a time his early moves toward adulthood, the grave looks and the knowing nods, were charming, even touching. After all, he was a kid and it was nice to see him practicing. But it had gotten old.

"I know that, Charles," I said. "Thank you."

"Well," he said. "I'm just trying to help. It's right, isn't it?"

Lily touched his shoulder. "Yes, Charles," she said. "But Dad's tired. Let's just be quiet and eat, what do you say? Dad's had a hard day."

"Another one?"

"That's enough, Charles," she said.

And it was. After that we ate in silence. I watched Christine, who did her corn first, kernel by kernel, then her beans. She didn't even touch her lamb chop after twirling it for the first five minutes. When I finished I took my plate to the kitchen, scraped it into the brown paper bag we kept under the sink—only the bag was out on the kitchen floor in front of the cabinet—and put my plate in the sink. I turned on the water for a few seconds to rinse the plate, then cut it off, went back through the dining area, stopped beside Lily to kiss her cheek, and went through the room toward the back door. "I'm going to straighten up out here," I said. "I may water for a while."

"You're going to water?" Charles said.

"Finish eating," Lily said. "I think your father might want his private time."

"What's private time?" Christine said.

"Don't be dumb," Charles said to her.

"Yeah, Christine," I said.

Lily looked up at me for a minute, then shook her head.

. . .

Out back a neighbor was setting up to barbecue. I didn't know the guy, just knew him to say hello, so I wig-wagged a greeting and then started messing with the Weber, working the vents, getting it out of the way. This neighbor had a red cooker. He had on a big T-shirt and balloon pants, and he spent a lot of time scratching his upper arms.

I watched him and thought I was living wrong. Everything was some kind of low-grade wrongness—things not quite fitting, feeling empty, feeling useless, without direction. I felt like I was stuck in the job, in the life, marking time until I don't know what, until I got older, I guess. I wasn't Mr. Imagination on the deal. Lily was great, a perfect companion, but she was a known quantity. I needed an unknown. Let's face it, a new woman stands for a new life, that's why men are always after them. The women don't like to think about that. A man falls for somebody and it's about escape nine times out of ten; the tenth maybe it's cooking.

So I was spending my fifth or sixth time thinking about the woman who was on *West 57th*, the TV show, when it was a TV show, the Wallace woman who wasn't even on there at the end, who went to cable, and then I was thinking about dewy young girls in the movies—though you don't see them as much as you used to, and when you do you don't care about them the way you did—and thinking of the semi-finalists who throng the malls. I wasn't thinking anything *about* these women, I was only thinking *of* them.

I put the charcoal lighter back into the storage closet and thought for a minute about sitting down in there. This closet was eight feet square, lined with the cardboard boxes our electronics had come in—computer, stereo, TV and VCR boxes, speaker boxes, the usual. I got one of the white wire chairs and put it in the storage room and sat down, my feet up on the bookcase that I got from the Storehouse so the closet would be more orderly—charcoal and lighter and chips on the bottom shelf, plant foods and insecticides on the second, plant tools on the third, electric saw, drill, and sander on the fourth shelf, accessories up top. It wasn't too bad sitting there in the closet.

I wondered if under my playful anger there wasn't real anger, no less real for being unconnected to bodily harm, or ignorance, or drunkenness, or dumb vengeance, no less real for being middle-class.

Newspapers and magazines said we had no business being angry. *Genuine* anger was the province of poor, ig- norant, violent people, people out of their lower-class heads, people driven by the elemental. Only poverty, cruelty, and abuse earned the large emotions. So they said, or wrote, but that seemed like money-guilt disguising a power- maintenance game. That made things easy to condescend to, easy to explain. Embarrassed by our collective good for- tune, the journalists redefined authenticity as the kingdom of the raw.

Making it a hard life for the non-poor.

If only I'd been cruelly scarred by father's heartless alcoholism! Terrified and violated by his vulgar, sex- spattered companions! Then I, too, could recall it today, put it to profit in a marketplace, sell high (TNT?), and thereafter moon about looking ashy and wounded in my Mercedes, in shy mint green.

From my closet I could see the untended brush and trees that bordered one corner of our lot. Lily always put plants out there in late summer—pencil cacti, euphorbias. Bud Patrick complained about this part of the yard because it bordered his. Now and again I'd see him out there trimming, careful to cut only his side of the fence.

I felt let down by my own bitterness. It wasn't glamorous and sacrificial, it was just business, fighting with clients, shrugging off what we did when we did bad work, which was more often than not. I suppose it wasn't all that bad, just ordinary, but it was bad enough to make going to the office depressing. If you take away the hope of doing something interesting, work becomes intolerable. Meanwhile there were bills—doctors, dentists, groceries, department stores, car people, insurance freaks, oil and gas guys, telephone bills and bills from the yard man, bills for dirt bought and bushes planted, bills for bathing suits and Mexican food, for heat and cooling and air to breathe, for clothes, toys, makeup, bills for the state, the city, the nation, for the enterprise. So I paid the bills, no more no less, in my sea of little failures.

And Charles—he brought a constant apprehension about the future, the schools he'd have to attend, the cretins he'd have to suffer, the way kids would isolate him if he dared hold an idea or opinion contrary to an idea or opinion of theirs, the pressures he'd face from teachers and students, the criticisms of the clothes he wore, the style of his hair, the brand of his shoes, and of his small hopes and of the tiny shadows of individuality he might display.

Lily walked right past the door of the storage closet out to the edge of the deck, looking around for me. "Peter?" she called. "Peter, where are you?"

"Back here," I said.

She turned and looked at me in the closet, saw what she saw, and said, 'What are you doing in there, Peter?"

I said, "Thinking about my sins," which was a thing my mother always used to say when I was a kid, that she was thinking about her sins. She didn't have any sins to think about, of course, which is why it was funny.

"Why don't you come out of there? Sit out here with me, O.K.?"

I said, "Fine," and picked up my chair and carried it back out to the spot on the deck where I had gotten it.

She closed the storage door behind me. "Now," she said, sitting down on the deck railing. "You've got this nice family, this nice kid and everything, this good job, and things are going great, right?"

"Things are O.K.," I said.

"Hallelujah," she said. "That's a big Amen."

"I'm trying to break on through to the other side," I said.

"Good," she said. "Just remember Peter Finch. In that movie, the one where he was mad as hell? I'm saying where'd it get him? I'm saying he's dead as a doornail, he's bad meat. He's two ears and a tail—I mean, there's a lesson in this."

I nodded. "You want me to get over it, right? You don't care what it is, how it is, if it gets handled or not, all you care is it's over, right?"

Lily smoothed her hair, then she smoothed mine and smiled at the yard. "Well," she said. "You're warm."

2

Charles came out of the house carrying a sleeping bag, a yellow ice chest, magazines, and the spread off his bed. "I'm camping out tonight, O.K.?" he said as he passed us.

I started to say no, but then Lily caught my eye and gave her head a sideways wag. This meant that she had already O.K.'d the venture.

"Watch out for spiders," I said.

"There aren't any spiders," Lily said, smiling at Charles and holding out her arm to him; he came over for a kiss, trailing his equipment.

I nodded. "That's right. No spiders. I just said that."

"Your dad's having a hard time," Lily said.

Charles was hanging around in an annoying way. It was as if he didn't really want to camp out in the backyard after all.

"I don't care about them, anyway," he said. "I play with spiders at school." He waited a second, then said, "Dad,

I'm making a tent. Is it O.K. if I use the boards behind the garage?"

I said sure.

. . .

It was dark and we had a pretty good tent in the yard. I was in there with Charles. He was reading a car magazine and listening to a tape on the portable we'd gotten him for his last birthday. I had already asked him to turn it down twice, and the second time he had gone inside for his ear-phones. It must've been midnight. I was lying on my back under the tent, my feet sticking out the back end of it, my head on one of the three pillows he had brought out. The floor of our place was cardboard, but we had a rug over that, a four-by-seven thing that Lily and I got at Pier 1 about fifteen years ago. I had gotten it out of the garage, where it'd been stored.

The bugs weren't too bad. Both of us had rubbed down with Off, so there was this thin, slightly turpentine smell in the air.

I got along well enough with Charles. We weren't like a *Father Knows Best* thing, but we did all right. He had his world and I had mine. Looking at him there in the tent, his head hip-hopping with music, his eyes on the magazine, I had an idea what he was about, what it was like for him. I mean, he saw the stuff I saw on TV and he believed it, or maybe he believed nothing, or maybe he recognized that none of it made any difference to him, anyway. I guessed that was it. And if that was it, then he was right, he was doing O.K. We had the yard, the bedspread-tent, there were crickets around there, and pretty soon the cat would stick its head in the opening at the front of the tent, look us over, maybe even come in and curl up. What went on outside, out in the big cities and the big streets, that was entertainment; it wasn't exactly that it wouldn't touch him, but that the scale was so big that in practical terms he was hidden. The country would do another Nicaragua, or another flag, or another abortion—just any other pathetic, ignorant joke—and he would be in school, or doing a desk job, or waiting for his second child. He was just like me, I figured; he was out of it. He could get in around the edges if he wanted to, he could be a TV guy, a reporter, a senator, a spokesperson—it was America, he could be anything, do anything, just as long as it fit right in. Maybe that was wonderful.

"What're you doing, Dad?" Charles said.

I kept looking at the top of the tent. "Thinking about you," I said.

"Oh," he said. He waited a minute, then he said, "Well? Is it a mystery or what?"

"It's no mystery," I said, rolling over on my side so I could look at him. He had the earphones down around his neck. "What're you reading?" I said.

"Bigfoot," he said. He flashed the magazine at me. It was called *Bigfoot*. "The truck, you know?"

"Monster truck," I said.

"Right. It's a whole magazine about Bigfoot—how they got started, what happened, you know. About the races and jumps and everything. Four by fours."

"You interested in trucks?" I said. What I was thinking was I didn't like the way this conversation sounded. It sounded like conversations on TV, fathers and sons in tortured moments. "Never mind," I said.

"I guess so," he said, answering me anyway.

"I don't know why I'm out here, Charles," I said. "Am I bothering you?"

"Not really," he said. "I mean, it's strange, but it's not too bad."

"I'm just a shade off track these last couple of months, know what I mean? I think I'm down on my fellow man—phonies, cheaters, liars, the usual. I mean, normally it doesn't bother me, I just play through. You do what you can. Pick up the junk and paste it back together whatever way you can."

"Dad? Are you drunk?"

"Nope," I said. "I haven't been drunk for years, Charles. There's nothing to drink about." I sat up, crossing my legs, facing him. "Listen, I have to tell you this, and I don't want you to take it wrong, O.K.?"

"O.K., Dad," he said.

"We're doing all right, right? I mean, you can handle this talk, can't you?"

"Sure," Charles said. "What?"

"Well, I thought I ought to tell you I never wanted to have a son, or any child, for that matter. I mean, it wasn't just a son I didn't want to have. Lily did. I didn't mind, you see. It's not like I hate kids or anything, it's just that having kids wasn't the great driver for me. You're a problem, you know?"

"I'm a problem?"

"Kids are," I said. "I mean, for me. I don't want to treat you like a pet, but you're small and sort of dumb. I realize that's of necessity and that it's changing—you're not dumb compared with other kids, but compared with adults, see? Actually, now that I think about it, you really *aren't* dumb compared with most of the adults I know. I don't mean dumb, anyway, but there's stuff you don't know, see what I mean?"

"Sure," he said. "I'm a kid."

"It's not stuff I can tell you," I said. "You just have to grow for a while, get older, learn it on your own type of thing."

"I'm ten," he said. "Dumb and ten."

"No, you're not, Charles. Not ten, not dumb. That's not what I meant, anyway. You're missing the point."

"Dad?" he said. "Are you sure you're O.K.? You want me to get Mom?" He was up, bent over, already on his way out.

"Well," I said. "Sure. Get Mom."

I settled down on my back again when he was gone. I felt fine, I felt O.K. In a minute Lily was crawling into the tent. "Peter?" she said. "What's going on? Do you feel all right?"

"I'm functional," I said.

Charles came back in long enough to get his magazine and his tape recorder. "I think I'll stay inside tonight," he said. "Too many bugs."

"I talked to him," I said to Lily.

"Uh-huh," she said. She had her arm across my chest and she was patting again. Usually I hated it when she patted me.

"So long, sport," I said to Charles as he backed out of the tent.

"Night, Dad," he said.

. . .

I was left there in the tent with my wife. I said, "I'm acting up, I guess."

"A touch," she said.

"But that's O.K., right? Now and then?"

"I guess so," Lily said. "But I wish you were clearer about it, the reasons. We're doing O.K."

"What's wrong is we don't have an obvious problem, something to make it simple. The good thing about misfortune, about being poor, addicted, cut up with a knife, sick with some high-profile disease, is that everything's easy as long as you're under pressure—it's easy to know what to do, what to think, how to act, what to feel. It's like TV. There are no additional complications. On the other hand you take us, no obvious problems, plenty of food, shelter, a healthy child, a decent life, house, cars, a future of some kind—we should be happy. But when things start to look O.K., the problems get intricate and insidious—it's not easy to figure things out anymore."

"So, I guess you'd prefer to be really sick, maybe in an iron lung or something? Maybe attached to a dialysis machine? Or maybe you'd like to have an untreatable colon streptococcus infection? Or give up a hand or an eye or something, just to simplify the situation?"

I gave her a Thank You smile. "No, but I would rather live on *Ozzie and Harriet,* or *Cosby,* or *Family Ties*—any of those. I mean, it'd be great to feel what those people feel, to have those clear troubles instead of just confusion. Those people don't have difficulty with depression, or money, or politics, they sleep pretty well all the time, they're wonderfully adjusted, they have some successes and they find the silver linings in their failures—they even have decent sex lives. Whatever they have, it works. It's hard to imagine Ozzie going crazy over some teenager he sees in tight cutoffs and a halter at the ball field, going home and jerking off in the upstairs bathroom fantasizing about this kid, about fucking her little teenage mouth. You don't see Robert Young doing that, either, or Meredith Baxter Birney on the other end of the ticket, going after some high-school jock she's been watching pump up every afternoon at the gym where she goes. It doesn't happen in their lives, but it's all over ours. We can't figure out which way is up half the time. We've never had a TV life, we don't feel that way, that settled, that comfortable. I mean, I'm forty years old and what have I got to show for it? A dinky house, a dinky wife, a dinky kid. When my parents were forty they had six hundred acres in West Texas, two houses and a bay home, four children, and a hundred friends—it was just like TV. At least that's what it looked like to me. I'll never get there."

"Dinky?" she said.

"A figure of speech," I said. "It's part of my complaint, huh? I've got to elaborate some. Forget I said it. So, anyway, I guess we're back where we started from."

"Yep. I guess we are."

"It's not a vague complaint," I said. "It's just that it covers everything. There're too many things to list. If you start listing things that are wrong and you try to do the job right, to really do a thorough job, you either make the things that are wrong smaller and sort of less wrong, or you go on listing things forever. You got forever?"

"Sure," she said. She waited a few seconds after she said that; I could feel her waiting. Then she said, "But I've got to go to the mall sometime."

"That's a joke, right?"

She got up on her knees and twisted around so she could lie down on her back alongside me. She took my right hand in her left. "See there? You got it. You're not completely gone. You're O.K. Maybe you're a little dinky or something like that, but you're still serviceable. We've just got to take it one thing at a time. We've got to go binary on this."

3 When we first met at a department store in Houston, complaining wasn't a big part of the deal. She was just out of graduate school on the East Coast, having been sent there by a culturing parent, and I had finished my first marriage and my first divorce. I was working in public relations, surprised how little there was to do—move contracts around, have meetings, listen to people's meager ideas punctuated by their dirty jokes. It was stuff I'd seen at my father's office as a kid, only then I thought it was just how they acted around me—I thought real business was something else.

I was at this department store hunting a gift for my mother's birthday; my mother was going to be seventy-one. Lily was stealing a purse. What happened was I saw her, she was pretty, I stopped to look and ended up doing cat-and-mouse with her, body-flirting, turning up unexpected. I followed her when she got on the escalator to go downstairs, and when we got out of the store I stopped her and introduced myself. I don't know what I was thinking of.

"Peter Wexler," I said, reaching out to shake her hand. Then I figured out she thought I was the store detective. She tried to give me the purse and something else she had in a plastic bag. This was an awkward moment.

I said my name again, refusing the purse.

"I'm Lily Mason," she said, finally holding my hand. "Hello. I'm a teacher, a substitute teacher." She paused, looked at me, then said, "I'm from outer space; we have no purses on our planet."

"It's that tough, huh?"

"You have no idea," she said. She was thin, but she wasn't frail—wiry, with mean skin and high cheeks, lots of shadows on her face, lots of bone.

We agreed to go for coffee, and settled on the Bean Barn, a narrow storefront in the mall next to an abandoned candy store. The place had three booths in peach leatherette and a couple of wire-topped tables out in the mall where people were trying to walk.

We took the final booth. I said, "Let's try again and start simple."

"You first," she said.

She had me. I said, "I do some PR, some consulting, live in an apartment, I'm divorced, and I've been thinking about my parents, about how they don't clean up after themselves. It makes me worry, like it's the beginning of the end and so on."

"What, because they don't clean up?"

I took a minute thinking about that. "Yeah, I guess it is an overreaction. They used to be so clean, though."

"Uh-huh," she said.

Then this guy in a badly stained and wrinkled jacket, a seersucker jacket, sat down with us. Out of nowhere. He had on khakis and this jacket that would have been at home at the Salvation Army, though I couldn't tell whether he was poor or putting on the Ritz.

Lily introduced him—his name was Ray and he was her brother. They lived together, at least for the moment, while he was short a job.

We shook hands and he hunched his shoulders and did a nerd laugh that was too close to home. He was a thick-necked guy, the sort if you looked at him you wanted to tie your boat off to him.

Lily seemed embarrassed. "Peter was talking about his parents," she said. "They're getting older."

"What's getting old is the neighbors boffing in the driveway," Ray said. He waved at the woman behind the counter for a cup of coffee, then turned back to the table, talking to Lily, ignoring me. "Last night again."

"Get serious," Lily said.

"I am," he said, making a hand gesture that looked like the Cub Scout salute. "Listen, I watch. Inside and out."

Lily was halfway between playful disbelief and exasperation, and I was trying to think of how to get rid of this jerk brother without making a jerk out of myself. I said, "Six months ago I helped my father build these shelves in the downstairs bath. It wasn't a big job, but it needed to be done so we did it. Then I come back and the saw is still on the floor in there. You'd think he'd have put it away, wouldn't you?"

Ray gave me a stupid look. "I'm talking sex in the yard and you want to talk shelves? Are your ears blocked or something?"

Lily said, "You're supposed to be discreet, Ray, turn away."

I liked that. I looked at her and felt lost, thought it

would never work, I wasn't going to get to first base. The clothes were too expensive. The hair was expensive. Maybe she stole the clothes, but the hair was a gift.

"Sounds like your dad's forgetful," she said, waving the subject away. "Our parents are that way, too, aren't they, Ray? They wear dirty clothes and swear they're clean."

"Personal hygiene loses the glamor at sixty," Ray said.

"Mine are seventy, both of them," I said.

He snickered. "At seventy it's all run-and-shoot. Mouse Davis didn't invent nothing." Ray was making a mess dipping his middle finger in Lily's cup and touching dots of coffee onto the Formica. His coffee had never come.

"A football guy," Lily said, patting her brother's arm.

"Mine play music," I said. "You're trying to sleep, or read, or take a quiet bath and here comes the Philharmonic through like there's no tomorrow."

"They probably don't hear so well," Ray said. "Anyway, what's the deal on all the quiet bathing?"

Lily threaded her fingers together, tapping her thumbs and looking out the tops of her eye sockets at her brother. She was doing Mister Rogers. "Do we remember what is next to Godliness?" she said. "Can we say—"

Ray said, "I guess they get annoying when they get old, don't they? Isn't that a standard thing?"

"I think maybe you're too rough on your parents," Lily said to me. "You resent them getting old and it takes the form of this hostility."

"Who's hostile?" I said. "I'm not hostile. It's Ray that's hostile."

"You got that right," he said. "I hate mine. Couple of old bags of wind as far as I'm concerned."

Lily shook her head, telling me that was wrong, telling me he didn't think that.

"Let me give you this babe in the driveway," he said, going back to his favorite subject. "She's straight out of a fuck show, some sex fiend."

"Sex fiend? Oh, Jesus Mary and Joseph. I don't think we have sex fiends anymore, Ray," she said.

"That's a damn loss," he said.

"The woman's a hundred percent Blue Bird Circle, anyway," Lily said. "She can't be a fiend."

Ray reached for and finished Lily's coffee. "Sometimes I sit there in my room at night with the light off and try to catch a glimpse through the cracks in their curtains—I mean, that's sick."

"No, that's fine," I said. "I've done that. It's not a problem. It's unremarkable, certainly not pathological."

"Who're you, suddenly?" he said. "Mr. Fabulous Anton Psychiatrist?"

"I think it's sick," Lily said.

"It's more than sometimes," Ray said. "It's all the time. I check them nightly."

"Well, maybe you'd better stop," Lily said. "That's all I've got to say."

4 For a week I kept missing her on the telephone, leaving messages that weren't returned, then she called one night, late. She wanted to know about me, so I told her, starting with the fifties in Texas, the dirty bop, the slop, the slide, spin-the-bottle and get-her-in-the-garage, and even though the music was the same, in Texas the fifties weren't about cultural adolescence so much as high grass and big sky. That's what I said.

"Real adolescence," she said. "Panties. I know what you mean. Same here. But it's a time thing, right? It's only now that the fifties have been turned into this big deal so everybody can recapture their shit—it's pathetic. Professors are at it, so you know it's dead."

"I figure they'll get tired of it and turn it back to us."

She said, "Everybody thought the future was going to be so marvelous."

I told her that where I had lived we had nothing as far as the eye could see, just grass that came up over your head, maybe four houses within BB-gun range, and that was it. A mile away there was a store, a wood-frame one-room grocery called Jax run by a guy named Jack. I explained about the spelling. Years later Jack died and his son Charlie took over the business, renamed the store Charlie's. Something was lost there.

"I see that," she said.

I explained that we didn't get TV until late because my father figured TV wouldn't last, and that the house wasn't air conditioned because air-conditioning wouldn't last. This was resistance to futurism, I told her. We had electric fans and tall glasses of ice water and breezes you had to imagine were blowing through the open jalousies.

"I'll bet the fall was great, though," she said. "Like when it first started getting cool? I wish I'd been around. What I remember is going to the lake, and the way boys smelled after they cleaned up in the locker."

"Oh?" I said. But I decided to let that go. I was thinking about kids I hung around with back then. There was the Roperson kid from two houses over—he lost a leg or something, then turned out to have a disease. No, wait—he lost an eye and had to have a glass one. He was a smart kid, too, so everybody felt bad about the eye. Some other kid lost the leg.

"I was a tomboy," Lily said. "For me every morning was paler and more blue than the last, every high cloud held the hope of a Sabre jet, every afternoon was about swinging over the bayou on a rope the thickness of your father's wrist, or sliding down into Mr. Bell's twenty-acre sand pit. On Fridays we always ate fish, trout to tuna melt to salmon puff. All genuine, too; we were the last pre-fishstick generation."

This talk went on, notes compared. Details kept coming back. I threaded my way from St. Orange School, through St. Anthony, and right off to college, then back to fall in love with a high-school girl, then to New York. "After a while you feel claustrophobic," I told her. "I remember going across the river to LaGuardia. Leaving. I remember looking out the back window of the cab. It was night. Things were glittering, wintry. The city was a stretch of high-spill lights and spun reflections, all blue-black, an album jacket, but I was glad to be going."

"Home," she said.

"Yeah, I guess. Anyway, I started liking crummy stuff. Junk stuff. Stuff that was ordinary. It was my rebellion against taste and class, my anti-esthetic period."

"Oh yeah," she said. "I had one of those. I went for Rod Steiger. I guess I went overboard."

"Anyway, I found out that bad stuff wasn't more—or less—interesting. These folks face-to-face with the big Sonys in their living rooms—you can't love them for a lifetime. Much less the wizard born-agains in their brightly colored so-modern condos with Stickley tables and art by recently important cactus painters."

"This was a Saint Paul thing, this realization? You, flung from the horse?"

"Maybe it was," I said.

Now she paused, kept me hanging, then said in a new voice, a nasal parody, tapping the time against her receiver, "An army of youth."

So I was figuring my next step while we talked, a meeting, a date or something. I felt like a dork-o-matic for going so slow. "Maybe we should go to a movie," I said. "I probably can't be boring in a movie."

"I hate people who say they're boring," she said.

"You're a tough room," I said.

"Thanks," she said.

"I want to take you out," I said.

"I know," she said.

There was silence on the telephone line. We listened to each other breathe. I waited. Finally I couldn't hold out, so I said, "O.K., so here's the deal. We'll go to dinner, Chinese, that's easy. I'll try to stop telling you everything that ever happened to me."

"Fine," she said.

"You should know that I do everything fast, almost everything—I eat, drink, sleep fast. This is a warning. I'll be offering you Egg McMuffins for breakfast, Whoppers for lunch, Colonel Sanders for dinner."

"All on the first date?" she said. "That's a lot of chow."

Then I was sure. I said, "Yes."

"Well," she said. "Do you, uh—like, believe that we live in a world born in a drive-through line, nurtured at an inflatable breast, reared in a coin-op laundry, and . . . parented by how-to book, educated by vending machine, dressed by mail-order, married by video, and sexed by telephone?"

"Jesus," I said.

"Say 'I do,' " she said.

"I do," I said.

She laughed. "I'm reading it. It's in this magazine I'm reading."

We set up a date that was supposed to be Chinese take-out in Briarwood, the subdivision where she rented a house, but ended up flight from Ray.

He let me in the kitchen door when I got there. "I suppose you want to catch up on the action," he said. "Well, she knows I'm looking. She must think I'm pathetic, the way she smiles. I'm sure that's what she thinks. Sometimes I run into her at the Stop & Shop and there she is smirking—it's horrible."

"Maybe she likes you," I said.

This idea seemed to surprise him. "Oh yeah? Maybe she wants to get in my garb? You think?"

"Sure," I said. "You're watching and she knows, right? She doesn't quit, close windows, pull blinds—you figure it. Tell her you find her attractive."

"You think I ought to talk to her? Try to get something going?"

"Write her a letter," Lily said.

She gave me a quick tour of her rent-house, then told me we were going out. She wanted to meet at the Conestoga

Party Club; she wanted us to take two cars. I didn't get that but said O.K., and when she pointed me back to the driveway and shoved my shoulders I went out and got into my car.

The restaurant was a windowless reconditioned Showbiz Pizza. I knew this Showbiz stuff wouldn't last. Or maybe they planned to do ten years and fold, get their profit and go, I don't know. Anyway, I'd been there once for a friend's daughter's birthday; all the games were played with aluminum tokens. These things were as thick as quarters, they cost a quarter, they were just like quarters, only they were tokens. I guess management figured if you bought ten bucks' worth of tokens you weren't going to cash in the leftovers—they probably had the market research to prove it.

When Showbiz went under the Conestoga people redid the cinder-block building into a bar-restaurant combo, but instead of installing windows, which would have been costly, they hired a Junior League realist to do a floor-to-ceiling mural of the great outdoors—white-tail deer, silvery fish leaping out of ponds, geese purling across the cobalt-blue sky, jackrabbits eyeing the customers. I guess the artist wanted to make a statement: the animals in the painting were all packing guns—rifles, pistols, automatic weapons. It was a real animal revolution in there.

When Lily arrived we took a booth next to a wall on which a couple of bandito squirrels, cartridge belts slung across their bare bellies, stood up on their haunches chewing pecans. We unwrapped our silverware. The napkins were small and as hard as tracing tissue. It was awkward at first. We studied the menus and placed our orders with a middle-aged woman in blue stretch, a woman who looked scientific, as if she'd been in the bottle too long. Then we looked at each other across the planks-in-urethane tabletop.

For a second I was worried we weren't going to have anything to say. It had been easy enough on the phone, but now I was thinking about picking up women, something I'd done maybe twice in my life, thinking what do you say when there's no reason to be together? Then I decided we'd picked each other up, but that wasn't much better, that just made us consenting adults.

Lily was eyeing the mural. "This reminds me of a TV show I saw," she said. "These guys were in a field, all lined up in a trench with shotguns and these big black paddles, and when the ducks got near enough the guys waved the paddles, like they were wings, I guess. The ducks were good-looking, dark against lemon-color streaks. Then these slimy guys started blasting birds out of the sky and what I thought was, you know, that's wrong."

"I know the feeling," I said.

"I wished the ducks had guns. I know it's sentimental, but the idea of blasting these fat guys, you know? It's pretty good." She made a jet fighter with her hand, diving it at the table and doing machine-gun noises. "I'd love to see that, a bloodbath, these nut scratchers scrambling for safety, falling over each other, splattering in the mud with the tops of their heads blown to smithereens. Like that Kennedy film. *Blam!*" She made an explosion sound and popped herself high on the forehead with a flat palm, rocked her head forward like Kennedy's.

"They'd shoot back," I said.

"We'd cut 'em down," she said. "We'd drill 'em."

She was looking in my eyes. I hate it when people look in my eyes. I mean, when they stare right at them, when I can see that what they're doing is looking right in there, because it means they want something, or they might find something, or it means they're going way off the beam.

I said, "You're *real* nice."

"What?"

"I said I like you a lot."

She got embarrassed, looked at the table. "I'm sorry," she said. "I guess I did too much on the ducks. I don't know what's wrong with me." Then she looked up, showing new resolve. "You want to just zip through dinner and go back to your apartment and be careful? No, that's wrong. I saw this show about the Peace of Mind Club. It's a safety club. You know, for sex. You're not a member, are you?" She traced an outline around a squirrel in the painting. "This is wrong, too, isn't it? I don't know why, sometimes I just get nervous. Forget all this, will you? I don't care about sex, really."

"Well," I said. "Fine."

She sat up, straightened her place setting. "O.K. Great. Can we just start again?" She tapped the wall. "Good squirrel," she said. "Let's talk about you, O.K.?"

I said, "We talked about me already."

"I am *so* sorry," she said. She was talking into the tabletop. "I do this. I need a verbal skill, just one. Jesus."

I said, "It's fine, really. What's your teaching like?"

"I hate it." She turned to look toward the cash register, drumming her fingers. "Of course I'm only a substitute so it doesn't matter. Anyway, I don't know why you'd want to hear about it."

I said, "Call me crazy."

"They've got people teaching you wouldn't let near your kid," she said. "Lots of them. I see the evaluations and all of them grade out superior. It's a joke. I mean, to hear them tell it they're all one in a million." She shrugged, shook her head. "I'm going to stop," she said. "I promise."

"It's O.K.," I said.

"So I had a fight with the guy in the room next to mine. He had the TV on all day. I asked him to quit it."

"TV?" I said. "You've got TVs?"

"You never heard of that? They're for PBS stuff, but we use them to sedate the kids."

I watched her. When the food came she quit talking and started eating. She held her knife wrong, like a pencil.

.   .   .

After dinner we drove in tandem to my apartment at Chateau Belvedere, an eighty-unit cedar-shake project buried in tall pines back off the highway feeder. It was almost one A.M. when we pulled into the parking lot, then walked up the hill to my block of apartments. I watched the wet sidewalk as we walked, listened to the wind chimes—lots of people out there had wind chimes. Two guys and a girl were in the laundry drinking beer and sitting on tables. One of the guys was real tall. My apartment was upstairs, a two bedroom with fur-brown shag and a low, mottled plasterboard ceiling. There was a crummy light fixture in the center of the ceiling in each room. I went to get drinks out of the icebox, and she sat down in front of the television.

I thought it was going pretty well. I hadn't been out much since the divorce, which I always called the first divorce, as if I expected others. When I had been out, mostly what I wanted to do was go home. Sometimes I thought I didn't want to get over my divorce at all. I knew I was supposed to, but I wasn't sure I wanted to. There's something seductive about being divorced, something safe and easy—like you've paid dues and you don't have to do what you're supposed to do anymore, you can go home and watch TV and do some scraggly cooking and not feel bad about it, like you're not missing anything. At the same time I missed almost everything about my wife and my marriage. I'd been so close to her that when I was around somebody else I felt like I wasn't where I belonged.

I brought beer for Lily, Coke for me. She sat at the end of the couch, her legs up and crossed under her, skirt punched down between her knees. I didn't look at her, I was staring at the channel changer that was on the coffee table. I was thinking I might pick it up.

"Why don't you tell me about your wife?" Lily said.

"You mean *that* wife?" I said, trying to think of what I could say about my wife that would be interesting and a little bit true.

"That's good," she said.

"Sorry," I said. I looked from her to the blank TV, then back. I was thinking about what I could say about my wife and I was looking at the coffee table trying to figure out if Lily thought it was a good coffee table or junk, and then I decided to go ahead and tell her something. I said, "The good stuff that has happened to me, most of it, most of the good memories of things being O.K., times that were fun and stuff, of an orderly world in which the right things happened at the right times in the right way, most of that stuff comes from her. I don't know why, but it's all hers."

Lily didn't say anything.

"I probably should have said that another way."

She went back to her bottle. "It's O.K.," she said. "It's interesting."

"No," I said, shaking my head. "It's not. It's not good. I mean, it's true, but now I think I'm going to be small and mean for the rest of my life."

"Well, that's better than being unctuous," she said.

"Wait a minute," I said. I was thinking about unctuous, about what a good word it was. Then I said, "I'll just go all the way on this. With her I felt like a child, but I don't feel like that anymore. It's as if I could only do that with her."

Lily nodded, moving her head real slow, waiting a minute as if thinking about what I'd said. Then she said, "I've got a fire engine."

I looked to see whether that was friendly or hostile; she wasn't smiling, so I figured friendly. I traced a knuckle on one of her hands. "What color?" I said.

.   .   .

It was a nice night after that. We made love and it wasn't a disaster, and then we went for a walk through the project. It was cool out there, damp, there were quiet stars in the sky. We stuck to the sidewalks and didn't say much, but after we'd gone through the place once, we were holding hands. I was comfortable. I hadn't been out in the apartment project for a while, other than coming and going, and I'd forgotten the odd comfort of being close to people with whom you have almost nothing in common, the community feeling even though you never talk to these people, and only rarely see them. I loved what it felt like to look down a five-hundred-yard line of apartments, cars parked in front, yellow street lamps dowsing the asphalt with little slicks of light, loved the pleasure of somebody pulling up across the street at two-thirty in the morning, a couple coming in from a party or a club, their too-bright, too-loud voices suddenly hushed when they see you. As we walked, heavy trucks soared by on the highway I could just make out through the trees. This wasn't a fancy project, but under the cover of night it was gently transformed into a place of small mysteries, of elegant shadows cast by young trees on badly painted wood siding, of the reassuring clicks and whines of air-conditioning compressors snapping on and cutting off, of the almost inaudible thump of somebody's giant stereo woofer—I could make out the music, I could picture the people, a young couple, turning up the wick any way they could.

Somebody screamed somewhere. It sounded to me as if it had come out of the woods, but Lily thought it had come from the other direction, from one of the apartments toward the front of the project, toward the highway. We stopped and stood perfectly still, listening.

In a minute she whispered, "Goner."

We started walking again. The grass alongside the walk glittered as we passed. Things were getting smoky out there. Lily and I went from hand-in-hand to arm-in-arm. She leaned her head against my shoulder. We stopped in front of a chip-filled garden to watch a gray cat spar with a twig, flip it up into the air, then catch it and roll over on its side and do Ray Leonard with its back feet. Even the fireplug out there was pretty good-looking—pale yellow with a lime-green top. We walked more and then ended up sitting on somebody's doorstep, facing the central courtyard of the project, watching the shining blue water in one of the pools through a chain-link fence. After a time Lily asked me if I was ready for sleep. I said I was. Going back toward my apartment I pointed out somebody's pretty, violet-lit bug zapper.

. . .

Lily was apologetic about breakfast. "I didn't mean to force you into anything," she said, pointing at the dishes on the table. "Eating and stuff."

She'd made breakfast while I was showering, and she

was self-conscious about it, about what it suggested or what it might suggest.

I said, "It was delicious," but I realized that sounded wrong, too formal. "I didn't mean that. I mean, I meant it was delicious, but I didn't mean the other part—you know what I'm talking about?"

"The repellent part?" she said.

That started me thinking again about how I really liked her. I thought maybe we fit together. Some real way, like people so old or ugly you can't imagine them passionate, or passionate together, or who look like they were passionate once and were done with it. I'd always wondered how those people got together in the first place.

Lily was clearing away the breakfast dishes. I watched the way she stacked. I liked it—she took most of the stuff out from between the dishes but left one utensil to separate them, to minimize the messing up of the bottom of the dish on top. I imagined her driving our kids to school, and then later, in the evening, serving everybody food picked up from Smok-A-Chik. I looked around the apartment and it looked a lot better than usual for the daytime. There was plenty of sun in there—white Formica and light-colored wood, plants in the windows. The TV was on, tuned to one of the morning shows, the sound low. Even the carpet looked O.K. The place had never looked that good to me before.

I figured if we were together we'd be like ugly people, or old people—stuck, satisfied. We weren't ugly or old, not yet, but we weren't young and pretty either; we were adults. If I had to say, I'd say we looked regular. She had good hair that was kind of soft and specked, a slightly troubled nose, the aggressive skin, eyes that brought the beach to mind. Maybe I was on the short side—just under six feet,

though well over the average height for American males—
and I guess I didn't help myself much with the jeans and
the pullover shirts, but my face was all right. People sometimes said I was ruggedly attractive, if that's possible for
somebody of my height. I had all my hair, but it wasn't
trained. It was brown hair. I wasn't the best judge of what
I looked like, but I was attentive, and I'd spent time studying
other men—in the movies, in the magazines, on the street.
I figured I had a look, I figured we both did.

.   .   .

When we were done with the cleanup she was standing in
the kitchen parenting her coffee, wearing only the dress shirt
I'd had on the day before. "In the morning," she said, "I
always feel like the day will never end. I used to hate morning. But then in the afternoon, I get scared there's not
enough time."

"There's not enough for me," I said. "You sleep O.K.?"

"Fine," she said.

"Was it cool enough for you?"

"It was pretty cool," she said.

I smiled my thank you. "Air temperature, I mean."

"It was fine," Lily said. "And I don't want to hear about
air-conditioning again. Or your father."

"I wish my father loved air-conditioning," I said.

"Amen," she said. "Let's go back to bed."

"We should go shopping, we should return to the site
of our meeting, commemorate everything. It's our first anniversary, right? A week and a half since we met."

"It's been the greatest week and a half of my life," Lily
said. "I swear it's true."

6

We went shopping. There were lots of customers. The mall was lovely to me, odd and pleasant and friendly—morning light sailing through new skylights, drifting around poised mannequins onto the baskets on display, onto water running in the mealy, too-blue fountain. My pleasure was all about Lily. "You want to buy when you're here, they've got that down," I said. "They really know how to do this. Buy or else."

"Or else what?" she said, fingering the freak-out graphics on the front of a hundred-dollar T-shirt.

"Just else," I said. I tucked two fingers into the waist of her jeans, pulling her away. "They seem very heavy in aluminium. I thought we did aluminium."

"*We* did," she said, feigning haughty. "Oh, forget it. Let's get a corn dog. There's a corn dog place in here somewhere."

"Maybe we shouldn't have come," I said. "Too many women here. It's a girl show. I don't think I can handle it."

"Yeah, I can see you've got trouble," she said, giving me a look that had defined itself quickly, overnight, a look that meant Earth-to-Peter. Then she pushed us onward to the corn dog stand.

I went along, but kept staring around. "See, like I see a pretty woman and she's selling shirts and first of all she comes up to me when I'm trying to look like I'm shopping for shirts and then she says, 'May I help you with something?' in that voice they teach them, the voice that says 'Would you like to fuck me now?' as if she didn't know, and I'm standing there at this counter staring down at a shirt that looks like it would fit a boy of fifteen."

"You're a big man," Lily said. "You need a man's size."

"Right. That's what I mean. I'm not a giant, not by a long shot, but I sure as hell can't wear these teeny little fag shirts you see everyplace."

Lily cocked a finger at me. "Oops," she said.

"Just an expression," I said. "Anyway, she's real pretty wearing this skinny dress made out of extreme miracle cloth, and the dress is bright, it's got wet-look reds and blinding yellows—a print you'd call grotesque on somebody's wife, but on this girl the thing looks like *Vogue* magazine, and she smells good, Jesus does she smell good, and there on her identity-tag it says her name is Peri or Caita, and when she repeats her question about helping you, you grit your teeth and look at her, but you get only as far as the lips— moist, flickering, almost smiling, almost carved, plum colored."

"Do you realize that your forehead is sweating?" Lily said.

I wiped at it with my palm. "I can't believe that my head does this," I said. "I don't know what's wrong with it."

"All right," Lily says. "All right. I understand. Maybe we'd better move along? She scares you. Leave it at that.

You hate her and she despises you, O.K.?" Lily had found the corn dog place and ordered a couple, one for her, one for me.

"She hates me?" I said.

"I made that up," Lily said. "Forget it. Actually she's probably very attracted to you in spite of the fact that your skull's a natural geyser. Even as she looks at you, her perky breasts heaving, she's imagining exactly what she'd like to use to dry your forehead, O.K.?"

The kid running the corn dog place came across with a couple of his very best, or so he said.

"What is this again?" I asked, when I had mine in hand and we were moving to a cluster of white benches. "I have never had a corn dog in my entire life, so I'm tender on, like, what it is."

"You ever hear of a hot dog?"

I nodded at her.

"Same thing," she said. She took off about half of hers at a bite, showing me the inside. "Ray's always talking about salesgirls."

"Oh, excellent," I said. "Me and Ray."

"Ray's O.K. He just seems freaky. He's nice, really. He says the girls are all automatics."

I shut my eyes and remembered a wonderful salesgirl I met once, a small girl with tiny cracks in her lips as she was talking to me, lips moving in slow motion, beads of moisture sliding slowly toward the corners of her mouth, the gloss of the whole lip structure lifting itself slowly to caress an utterance, an invitation in a steamy corridor. We had coffee and then I gave her a copy of *Being and Nothingness*, my name and phone on the inside front cover in hopes of enticing her to call.

"Is it O.K. if we just forget about it?" I said.

"Fine," Lily said. She was winding up, straightening and stretching, and then she said, "O.K., I think I should tell you this."

"What?"

"I stayed up with Ray and watched the neighbor woman screw. I've never seen anything like it. She's got the mouth of a gar."

"Standard equipment," I said. "No news there."

"I felt bad after," she said. "I don't think you're supposed to watch. I think that's a neighbor law."

I said, "This one here's pretty cute," pointing out what looked like a nine-year-old, a girl in bike pants and a wish-top.

"This isn't our best moment so far, is it?" Lily said.

We stopped talking then, watched shoppers go by, watched and waited for something to change our conversation, our mood. I figured we needed two minutes to get out of the death spiral.

So I said that to her.

She said, "Oh, great. Already? So you want to talk more about the parents? I don't know what you're worried about."

"That's not what I'm worried about now," I said.

"No, now it's us, right? I've seen this movie before, I know this trick. There's the matter of what you want with me, a subject we've sidestepped."

"C'mon, Penny, take it easy, will you?"

"I hate that," Lily said. "Why'd you call me Penny? Are you making fun of me or what? Because I can make fun of you, too, if I have to. You and your shirt girl."

I said, "Would that be sort of like watching people fuck when they don't know you're there? Is that TV with the sound off, only real?"

"TV's real," she said.

"Got me," I said.

"Fine," she said, giving me impatience. "But I'm talking sex, now. Even if they're not doing anything, you know, even if they're washing dishes, if they're reading or something, you're like waiting for them to get going. It's sort of fun. It was strange with Ray—you should have been there. Then later I went to bed and it was like I'd made it up, I think I wished that I had made it up. I wasn't sure they'd been there at all, out there, wasn't sure I'd seen them making love. It was dark, and there was the fence, there were bushes, I was afraid to open the window too much. I mean, I thought I should for the sound, but if I opened the window they might hear. They might even stop, go inside, something."

"So you sat there with your brother and watched."

"You couldn't see a lot. I was thinking the streetlights would help but they didn't because they were too bright."

"I don't think it's good for you to do stuff like that," I said.

"I only had my curtains open half an inch so I could only look out one eye at a time, which made it hard to get the whole picture." Lily was staring off into the mall, the waxed paper that had come with her corn dog crinkled and motionless in her hand, held there like a caught gray cloud. "I don't want to talk about this anymore," she suddenly said. "I don't like it and I'm sick of it."

"That does it for me, too," I said, stuffing half my corn dog and its waxed paper into a brown, open-topped garbage can. "What next?"

. . .

What next was a walk, window-shopping, and a feeling that we liked each other again. "I don't really want to, but if you want to we can dump Ray and hang over at my place, wait for the show. Before you know it there she is driving into her driveway, smiling, late afternoon sun glinting in her hair."

"It glints in yours," I said.

"We could get binoculars, I guess." She shook her head as if tossing off the remnants of the idea. "Well, it doesn't matter. The suburbs are lovely at night though, don't you agree? The neatly laundered homes and the prim grass and the friendly dogs wandering around like interplanetary travelers, and the white moonlight splitting tall pines—are those pines at your apartment?"

"Pines are sticky," I said. "You touch their trunks and they're sticky."

"And all the car washing that goes on in those pretty concrete driveways in the early evenings—don't you love that?" Lily said. "None of those people want to hurt you."

"I always wanted to live in Florida," I said. "The Gulf Coast, where the water's green. I'd like to see you in that water. I'll bet you're amazing in the water—like TV ads."

"What? What's that mean? You think so?"

We took a left into the part of the mall where the department store was. I said, "I was surprised when I saw your house. It's nice, but it's ranch style, right? What does that mean, anyway? Ranch style?"

Her skin was acid perfect. It killed me.

"It means spread out, I think," she said. "The rooms are all spread out like the pastures on a ranch."

"No kidding? That's amazing. I never knew that."

"That's what Ray says, anyway." She stopped me, held me at arm's length. "I get the feeling you're tired of this. You seem foggy, like you've lost track of things."

"I may have lost track of your things, but I certainly haven't lost track of mine," I said. "Why'd you say that?"

"I was just sharing a bit of a personal feeling with you."

"You were?" I said.

"I was showing it to you," she said. "I was letting you get the sense of it without really really saying it out loud."

"What was it again?"

"Ray," she said. "It's odd living with him, but I don't mind. I was wondering, though, if you wanted me to meet your parents, you know, so I could see what you're talking about and everything. I think that might be a good idea."

"Meet my parents?" I nodded. "Sure. But you probably wouldn't find them interesting, nothing but age—they want to teach, they want to explain, they want to help. The usual. They're having a hard time of it because nobody wants to listen anymore. They don't even want to listen to each other—it's horrible."

"Still, if I met them, sort of put myself in your shoes . . ." She patted my arm.

"That's what you're thinking all the time?"

"Just today," she said. "Last night and today."

"Oh," I said.

"Don't get scared," she said. "Everything's tip-top. Maybe we could drive around awhile, talk over a few things, your father, your women, pretty women." She gripped me tighter, holding on to my arm with both of hers. "My damaging personal sexual failure, the window and that, and you'll want to talk more about the women in the stores— they are unsparingly gorgeous, aren't they? All these young women out here in the mall right now, slew foot and poised, haunting our perimeter. Hear them?" Lily's face was up on my shoulder now, she was whispering close to my ear; I felt her breath. "They're circling, Peter, circling, breathing that sweet breath of theirs, lather rising on their flanks, they're pawing the carpet and dripping with the scent of a thousand distant fires. They're coming."

held unthinkable jobs—for a while he imported parrots from South America. One of his ex-wives was 1984's Miss Uruguay, so he had the inside line on Uruguayan parrots, which, according to him, were among the finest parrots in the world. He also sold fur coats out of his apartment during this time, had people over for drinks and showed them "hundreds of thousands of dollars" worth of coats. He did this trick with his favorite parrot where he took the parrot outside and put it on its back on the sidewalk then walked away—a variation on the bullfighter tormenting the bull. Ray called it their "playing dead" game, but when he finally showed it to me, the bird opened one eye as Ray moved away, as if judging the distance between itself and him, then suddenly spiraled straight up and disappeared into the sky. After that Ray quit parrots and coats, and teamed up with a guy from Iran selling water by telephone for a living. All he had to do was get the order and FAX it to a water depot he was hooked up with on the North Side. He met a lot of women he liked and who liked him, and he always brought them by to meet Lily and me; they were always good-looking. There was some cowgirl mystic from Alabama for a while before the Mistress of Uruguay, and most recently he'd moved to California with a woman who sold blue-eyed tiger paintings out of her van on Sunday mornings in abandoned gas stations. That hadn't worked so well out there, apparently, and now he was coming back without her. Meanwhile, we'd had the usual allotment of young married experiences—the problem parents, the money trouble, the cats, cars, a second mortgage, more credit cards, the insurance, tuitions, dues, doctors, plumbers, counselors, orthodontists, lawyers, tree surgeons, mechanics, bug people, and more than our fair share of misguided furniture. I think we were suckers for bad furniture since that day we met in the mall. I adored Lily, though the adoration was more complicated than it had been at first. The same went for Charles. Lily changed jobs a couple of times, doing well, finally got out of teaching altogether and into arts administration.

My working life hadn't gone as I might have liked. It was worse than that, really. Not that I wasn't successful, I was. I made enough money, moved up, switched companies until I got into facilitation consulting, where I stayed. We did what people needed doing—travel, meetings, software, PR, promotions. This was one of those new-idea companies that actually caught on even though it wasn't so new once you took the wrapping off—specialties is what we did. Anyway, I fared well enough there, but I liked it less every day. It seemed as if everything had gone south on me, not in any clearly defined way, and maybe not even so much in the way things were, but in the way I saw them, in my outlook—I'd become, according to Lily, cranky and parsimonious and unkind. The last was her way of telling me I was way off base; to her, being unkind was the worst, the most unforgivable. "There just isn't any reason for it," she'd said.

"You're awfully well-adjusted," I'd said.

"Hey," she said then, waving both hands at me crisscross style about ten inches away from my nose. "Wake up. The fifties, sixties, seventies, and eighties are over. You've been in the shelter too long, boy."

8 A couple of weeks after my talk in the tent with Charles, Lily and I decided that maybe we'd better spend some time apart. It was pretty much my idea, my decision, although Lily said at first that she thought it was an O.K. thing. "We've been having this anger trouble for a while," she said. "Maybe if we get away from it things'll straighten out."

This was at dinner. I'd just finished telling Lily and Charles all about focus groups, about how I hated them. "There's something fundamentally wrong with focus groups," I said. "They're inhumane and nondiscriminating. I don't know why we always sit still for the phony social science junk. And it's worse the last couple of years. Sometimes stuff is so squalid and low you just want to go up on the tower like what's-his-name did down in Texas."

That's where she stopped me. "Peter?" she said. "Can you hear what you're saying? Starkweather Syndrome."

"Whitman," I said. "Besides, I didn't mean it. I'm sorry. I apologize. I'm not climbing any towers."

"It's fantasy," she said. "You're painting with the big brush again. You're using the paint that's shot from guns."

. . .

We'd had a "move out to the garage" joke ever since we got the house, but neither one of us had ever gone. We kidded about it all the time—sometimes she was supposed to move out, sometimes I was. It was a running thing. We had a two-car garage with the apartment above—we'd redone the apartment when Lily was planning a home office. We'd gotten the tight carpet, industrial gray, the cheap plastic blinds that look like Levolors, Wal-Mart's good white paint, and then, when the office idea went up in smoke, we used our discardable furniture to fix the place up like a guest cottage.

In the middle of the next day I said, "Maybe I could move out to the garage for a while. Treat it as an apartment."

"Maybe you could," she said.

"I'm thinking about doing it today," I said.

Lily didn't want to help me think about that, so she decided to go to the store. "What do you want for dinner?" she asked.

I'd already begun sorting clothes in my head. "Vegetables," I said. "I'm going on an all-vegetable thing."

"I don't know what they have that's fresh," she said.

"Who cares?" I said. "Fresh doesn't know my name. Get frozen junk—corn, lima beans, black-eyed peas, rice—that's what I want. Birds Eye. Maybe it'll modernize my system."

"Rice is not a vegetable," she said, heading for the door. "I'll get a steak in case you change your mind."

"I'm not changing my mind," I said.

"I know that," Lily said.

Charles was out front working on the sidewalk with the edger. He was another part of the problem—since our talk he'd kept his distance, and Lily was always listening in. I'd be talking to Charles and catch her leaning around a corner to hear what we were saying. I kept telling him stuff I thought he needed to know. She told me I was doing just what my father had done.

"You're more like your father every day," she said.

"It could be worse," I said. "I could be one of these lost-to-the-pan guys who wash their cars in driveways every afternoon, who look like kids ready for church when you see them out with their wives—the Stepford Guys."

"You're always ready for church," she said. "Besides, our life was built on washing cars in driveways, what're you talking about? You loved it."

"Yeah, I know," I said. "I miss it, too."

She shook her head and looked at the ceiling as if offering a prayer. "Hormones," she said.

Then we had this odd, tough, quick talk in which I said I was tired in a new way, and she said she was waiting me out. I loved her ferociously for that. I told her that something had snapped, that I didn't know what. She said that was just marriage. She said she had all the time in the world, that she was made of time. I said I might actually go, move out, that I couldn't stand always feeling depressed and angry, and I didn't know what to do, I was flailing. She said, "Flail away," and then she left for the store.

.   .   .

In minutes she was back for her shopping list. I had gotten it off the kitchen counter and noticed that it had at least six misspellings on it. I corrected the misspellings. It was a habit

I had, correcting her shopping lists, a habit she didn't like. I didn't correct the intentional misspellings, or the pet words she had for things—like *yeggs* for eggs, or *mlik* for milk— just the things I knew she was trying to spell right. Sometimes I'd try to correct words and then couldn't figure out how to spell them myself, so there would be a lot of crossed-out stuff on the list where I'd tried a couple of times to spell a word. Whenever I couldn't spell one I just left it off and scratched out my misspellings thoroughly so nobody could see how pathetic my attempts had been. Lily didn't complain about this habit of mine anymore. She was fine on the brand names, it was the generics she couldn't handle. She hadn't spelled "raisin" correctly in the fifteen years I'd known her.

We had argued about me correcting her—not only spelling, but grammar and pronunciations, titles she got mixed up, actors, product names, pronoun references— there were lots of things Lily never got the hang of, so I was forever correcting, which wasn't particularly fun for me, either, only I couldn't stop. She was the one who figured she could make intentional mistakes and throw me off track, and that worked for a while, so we kept that in. The shopping list was about all I tried to fix anymore.

On her way out with the list she stopped by the door and said, "Listen, are you serious? About moving?"

"I don't know. Yes, I guess. I don't think I'm fit company."

"So take it out on me, right? Punish me?"

"Of course not," I said.

Charles stuck his head in the door to ask if I thought both sides of the sidewalk needed trimming or if he could just do the side he hadn't done last time and that way even things up.

"Fine," I said. "Do whatever you think is right."

He made a fruitcake face at Lily and said, "Pardon me for living," then let the door shut behind him.

Lily said, "So why move out if it's not my fault? Is this we live together so I'm implicated, even if I'm not doing it myself?" She nodded to herself as if suddenly getting the point. "Oh, yeah. I know this drill. You hate to hear my voice, sometimes, right? You hate the way I look in my shorts or something. Hate it more than usual, I mean. You probably even hate that I understand that you hate these things."

I leaned my head back against the wall and said, "No," staring at the light fixture.

"And this is the fault of the external world, correct?" She shook her head, not waiting for the answer. "This is so stupid. I know everything you do before you do it."

"You knew this?" I asked.

"Sure. I've become too *present* in your life."

"I think I should spend time alone," I said.

"Not again," she said.

"Things are messed up and it's getting worse. I want some relief and I'm not getting it here, not under these circumstances, and so I'm not doing you or Charles any good. I'm telling Charles all this stuff that seems absolutely true to me, and I'm telling him even though I know he shouldn't have to hear it."

"Yeah, you've got it rough," she said. "Tote that bale."

"Please, Lily. I know how rough I haven't got it, O.K.? You don't have to remind me."

"We'd be better off if something really terrible happened to us," she said. "Like to one of us or something. Then we wouldn't have to go through all this silliness of separating, worrying about how we feel, about how happy we are or aren't. I mean, most people don't do this, Peter. They buckle down."

"Yes, Mom," I said.

"Besides, this breaking up isn't stylish anymore. Nobody does it. You're supposed to shut up and stick together now, like the old days."

"Right up until the eve of the divorce," I said. "Then do it quick so nobody notices, so there's no time between being married and being single."

"You're thinking about divorce?" she said.

"That's not what I meant," I said. "I was commenting on the rest of them, the *others*."

"Oh," she said. "Them." She did a parody of a dismissive gesture. "Well, you're a handful for me, don't forget that. And Charles is a big crowd. We're all about equally disaffected, O.K.?"

"This isn't about disaffection or disconnection or dysfunction, it's about hiding. I don't want to be in the middle of stuff anymore, you know? I want to cocoon, to hide from these pathetic drooling dicks, these creeps who believe the butt-juice they prattle about."

"Sorry I asked," Lily said, waving her hands in front of her and making a bad-smell face. "Now, remind me again how moving out is going to fix this problem?"

"It's a change, *change*," I said. "It's something. Maybe it's enough."

"What is this, Peter? What's the deal? You sound like Ray."

"I wish," I said. "Hey, I'd go down if I could. If I had a chance I'd be the first one into my cardigan. I promise. I'd be out there on the lawn. I'd be standing there, hitching my trousers, waiting for a neighbor with whom to discuss some of the serious issues. But I can't, quite, so spare me the homily. The folks aren't going to let you on in prime time to say what they already know, that bankers *are* the drug problem, that searching TV shows *are* the problem, that our need for the problem is the problem, that the problem is guys with the brains of rodents in the streets, million-dollar guys, with the brains of rodents, on TV, and very educated professorial types, with the brains of rodents, on our campuses. Or to say that money is the big engine that could, that money wets your pants and your whistle with equal vigor, or to say that kids don't care about their parents, that the idea of parenting is so outdated that its stylishness only ensures its uselessness, except as a protection for us and the kids, so we all have something to hide behind while we flee each other, or to say that professions are run by fart-kissing careerists, managers, bureaucrats, and dimwits, and our fellow beings are narrow, unimaginative, uncaring, lying queer-bait sons-of-cunts, and that the worst possible things you might think about others are usually about half as bad as the true things, and so on, and so on, O.K.? Even if they let you say all this stuff, who would want to hear it? And the TV bozos know that, too, so they might give you a show of your own, just to demonstrate how open they are to these new ideas. And yes, I know people have said exactly these things for years, and that nobody wants to hear it because it's *so* negative and harmful to our self-esteem, which is more important than truth now that truth isn't worth the paper it's printed on because it's conveniently undiscover-able, not to say that it's unclear, unmarketable, and it doesn't go on TV very well, except in bad time slots when bad people are watching, after all the good people have gone to bed, or when they're off at work having meaningful human relations with their peers and colleagues, et cetera."

"Is that it?" Lily said. "It seems like you're sputtering, here. Like you're running down."

"I'm not. I'm pulling punches."

"Oh yeah? Why would you do that? There's nobody here but us chickens."

"I don't know why I would do that," I said. "I just always do."

"Maybe that's the problem," she said. "Maybe that's what you ought to think about when you move to the garage."

. . .

I watched her back out of the driveway thinking she was going to get the mailbox this time for sure; I was wondering, too, if I should get Charles to help me get my junk out to the garage. I thought I could explain to him what was going on, why I was moving, while we were doing it, and then I thought maybe I wouldn't, because it wouldn't come out clear and he was too young, anyway. I didn't know why I wanted to explain stuff to him—I guess I wanted to win him over or something, but I didn't know why that seemed necessary. Besides, the only thing Charles approved of was a local band called Tug Butter and those small motorcycles called bullet bikes, which he called crotch rockets when he wanted to get my goat. I let him have it; in fact, whenever it came up, I played along by doing a self-serving, self-righteous, hateful, low-road Pat Buchanan imitation, just like on TV. Charles loved it.

For a few minutes after Lily was out the driveway I watched Charles working along the edge of the sidewalk. I stood at the window and watched and then, when I thought enough time had passed so he wouldn't think it was a put-up thing, I went out there after him. It was hot outside, a dull heat, and I remembered times when my father sent me outside on new fall days to do what I didn't think needed doing. My father was a cattle drover when it came to getting mileage out of a kid. I hated it back then, but it made good work habits and all the rest of that. I went to the office and then came home and worked until it was time for bed; I did that probably because that's what he did, and that's what he had me do when I was a kid. He did carrot and stick stuff, too—do this and this, and then you can do that—and so I did it to Charles, too, sometimes. Anyway, as a kid I worked while my friends rode around in borrowed convertibles. My friends peaked out in high school, where they excelled in sports as well as academics; I don't exactly know how to describe what happened to me.

I tried to imagine that Charles looked like me, looked the way I must've thirty years ago, but I couldn't see it; I was a towheaded guy in hand-me-downs, a kid with that late-fifties look about me, insulated the way the world was then. Charles looked like a small Magnum P.I., or somebody they were thinking about for the next Bond film—he handled the edger as if he were taking fingerprints off it. Or maybe he just wanted a Weed Eater like all the other kids on his block. Either way, I guessed this could be called cultural progress, the *new day* as played out in neo-domestic neo-realism across the land.

On the sidewalk I went around him, giving him a wide berth, and then planted myself in his way, so he couldn't avoid me. I wiggled my arm at the edging tool telling him to put it down.

"What's wrong?" he said, looking up the sidewalk at the edge he'd already done. He had the edger head-down in the dirt, and he was leaning on the handle like a young

Jack Nicklaus—he definitely didn't belong to me. "I guess I screwed this up, huh?"

I thought that I didn't want the part he pushed me into, that I wasn't old enough to have a son like him, that it seemed only a few months ago, a year at most, that I was headed out to the meanest bar in town to play rock'n'roll with really bad guys. And the majors were interested; they sent people down.

"No," I said to Charles. "It looks fine. It looks real good."

He eyed the sidewalk and then me, as if to ask if it looked O.K. how come I was stopping him. He had things to do. He didn't have time to stand around chatting.

I said, "Let's take a walk."

It was pretty clear he didn't think that was the best idea he'd ever heard. Something about the way he moved his shoulders, curled them over, crablike. "It's hot, Dad," he said.

"Never mind that. I want to explain something. Something I've been thinking about."

He was still there with the tool poised, so I took it from him and dropped it in the grass alongside the sidewalk. Then I put an arm around his shoulder and turned him toward the garage. There was a path around the side of the garage by which we could get into the backyard. I wanted to have this talk in the backyard.

"In the first place, Charles, what you ought to do when I come up and say I want to have a talk with you is say O.K. I mean, the way you look here is *Why doesn't he leave me alone?* That's fine sometimes, but not now. I'm your father. I'm not trying to be your father, I just am, you know? So, I mean, if I want to talk to you then you should try to say O.K., O.K.?"

He said, "I'm sorry, Dad."

I thought I had him, so I drove on. "It's fine, not a problem. What I want to tell you is that there are all these things wrong now that were not formerly wrong. I'm figuring you're going to notice that they're wrong and start wondering why, so I thought I'd get a step up, you know? Doing my duty and everything. I'd really like to tell you that things get better as you get older, life and stuff, but they don't, usually."

He looked uncertain, so I said, "Let me give you an example. I was sitting inside here thinking about a war with the Japanese. Now, Charles, we're not about to have any war with the Japanese, you understand that, right?"

"We're friends with the Japanese," Charles said. "They give us all our stuff, don't they? They make master bikes."

"Right," I said. "But they're a different people than we are, and you get your wars a lot that way. But that's not the point, anyway." Charles was having trouble sticking with me, I could see that. He was more interested in his feet, in the careful placement of his feet as we walked, than in what I was saying. For a second I remembered something about what it was like to be a kid, but the memory went by so fast that I was not certain I really remembered it at all. That threw me and I had to make an effort to keep talking. "See, if we were to go to war with the Japanese—let's say we were going to do that—and let's say the Japanese were winning and came over here and took over part of this country the way the Germans did in Europe in World War II, or like we did in Vietnam—you know what I'm talking about?"

"Yes, Dad," he said. "You mean, like, liberating the country, right? Like saving it from itself?"

I stared at Charles and realized that I didn't know where

he got that—I didn't know what he knew, what he meant. Was that TV? Or was it just in the air by now? I said, "So, I was thinking if they were here I'd help them." I waited a minute to see how he was taking that, but he didn't react. "You're not supposed to—you know that?"

"Sure. They'd be the enemy."

"I mean, Charles, I wouldn't help them kill us or anything, but I'd cooperate. And the reason—you want to know the reason?"

"Sure, Dad. Why would you help?"

"Because although there was a time when this was a wonderful country and we did everything right—or that's what everybody thought, everybody who lived here, anyway—that was a while ago, and now it's clear that we're maybe somewhat less wonderful than we had hoped."

"They say we're still the greatest," he said. "I hear that all the time."

"Ali says he's still the greatest," I said. I had this feeling that I wanted to touch Charles, to hold him, press his body against mine—father and son stuff, but much stronger than usual. "Maybe that's a bad analogy," I said, thinking it over. "Ali probably is still the greatest. So that's a different thing."

"We're not as bad as Iran, are we?" Charles said.

"We're friends with Iran now, Charles."

"Yeah, but I've seen *those* people on television and they're a lot worse than us. They've got cool hair, but they're always smacking themselves over the head. With chains and stuff. That's dumb."

"Yes," I said. "Hair is a national tragedy over there."
"What?"

"Joke," I said. "It's a hair joke. It's shorthand. You know about shorthand, don't you?"

"I guess so," he said, but I could see that I'd lost him. He looked at his pants and flicked away a slice of grass caught on one perfectly creased trouser leg.

.   .   .

The backyard was like an abandoned place. I could see fifty things that needed doing, but I told myself it was more important to spend this time with Charles. On the other side of the collapsed chain-link fence that separated our yard from Bud Patrick's yard there was Bud himself, doing what he likes to call his weekly malingering. According to him it's a word he invented. This week he was malingering with his satellite dish—he had the leg that sticks up toward the center of the dish sprung loose and he was working on the horn part.

I motioned that Charles should sit on the edge of the patio and I perched on a sawhorse that was standing there. "The Japanese are a lot like us, Charles. They're like what we used to be—I mean, they practice what we used to preach. They work hard. They get a job and they try to do it right. I'm not saying that every Japanese person in Japan is that way; in fact, I read something a few weeks ago about Japanese workers wanting to be more like our workers. That sent a chill down my spine. Still, some of them, maybe most of them, have figured out there's a percentage in doing good work. We haven't figured that out over here yet."

"Sure, but we're a lot more democratic than they are," Charles said. "They have these little tiny houses and they're not very democratic."

I had one eye on Charles and the other on Bud Patrick, and I wondered if the backyard was such a good idea. Bud was a friendly guy. I said, "What, Charles?"

"Well, we vote and everything. You can do anything here. Guys argue right out in the open, like on TV."

Bud saw us and headed for the fence. I gave him a wave hoping that would satisfy him, keep him on his side.

Charles said, "At dinner, you know, when we switch between that show on the news thing, you know the one? And the one on the other channel? I listen to those guys sometimes. They argue, don't they?"

I said, "They pretend to."

"You mean it's fake? All that time they're yelling and stuff?"

"Well, not exactly. One guy takes a position and usually distorts the other guy's, and if the other guy argues back, then the first guy repeats the distortion. This is the current definition of argument. But you see they aren't arguing, right? It's first-strike stuff. The idea is get on louder and quicker, and repeat more, so the viewer remembers you and not the other guy."

"Oh," Charles said, thinking about that as he got up, brushed off. "I mean, is that right? I always thought you were just saying it." He pointed back the way we came around the house. "O.K. if I finish up out front?"

"Wait a minute," I said, grabbing his shoulder. I wrapped an arm around him in a fatherly way, a way that seemed fatherly, even though I knew what I was doing was restraining him, keeping him from going back to his edging.

Right at that point Bud said, hollering from his side of the fence, "So, what's up with you two? Am I interrupting?" He was starting to climb the fence and it was sagging under his weight. He was almost over the top, standing with one foot squeezed into a broken link and the other on the top bar of the fence—he was ready to vault into our yard.

"How's it going?" I said, waving toward his yard.

"I'm working on my dish," he said. He hitched his khaki shorts, his knees knobby and white like a just-rinsed turkey. "You gotta get one of these things. They're great." Just then his phone rang and he tried to jump back off the fence, but his foot was caught and he buckled on it, fell, twisting his ankle and ending up on the ground on his side of the fence with a leg knotted in the loose chain mesh.

Charles was faster than I was getting over there. "Are you all right?" he said, hopping the fence and squatting beside Bud, starting to peel the fence away from Bud's leg.

"Don't touch the ankle," I said.

"He's not touching me," Bud said, flat on his back and doing a hand-pistol at Charles, keeping a stiff upper lip. "Your dad giving you trouble?"

"We were talking," Charles said.

There was an eight-inch scratch along the inside of Bud's pink-white left leg above and below the knee, and the scratch was doing a lot of bleeding.

"You want me to get something for the cut?" I said, pointing at his leg. "Is it sprained or anything?"

"I'm fine," Bud said. "Put peroxide on this baby and I'll be super." His phone rang for a fourth time and then quit. He waved it off.

I sent Charles inside for peroxide and bandages, and then I sat down in the grass on my side of the fence opposite where Bud was stretched out. The grass was amazingly soft and cool. I felt as if I could sleep there.

"You guys having a heart-to-heart?" he said, fingering the blood a bit. He shrugged. "I guess I've been watching. It's hard not to, you know."

"It's nothing," I said. "We were talking about the junk that's going on these days."

"Yeah? What junk?" he said.

I felt like I had trouble right there. This was not stuff I wanted to talk about with Bud Patrick. I said, "We were talking the usual—TV, newspapers, the mayor. Kid stuff."

That didn't slow him down at all. "Degeneration of family values," he said. "That's the issue that's got me worried."

"It's big for me," I said, checking the house to see if Charles was on the way. He was coming through the sliding patio door. Bud was still on his back, but I didn't think there was anything very wrong with him, I didn't think he was hurt.

"Still," he said. "We're doing better every day. A bit better."

"Maybe so," I said. "I guess sometimes it seems that way."

"It's better," he said, sure of himself.

I watched Charles hand over the peroxide, a tube of Neosporin, gauze pads. When he backed off I stood up and wrapped an arm around his shoulder, which felt broad, solid for a kid his age. "I was reading this article about Russia," I said. "This is the new Russia, right?"

"Sure," Bud said. He was sitting up, dousing his leg with sizzling peroxide.

"So whoever wrote it said 'It's an amazing thing, this new openness. It even extends to the State. Even the government speaks the truth.' "

"That's right," he said. "Beats the hell out of me."

Charles was watching Bud doctor his scratch, which was much meaner-looking after the peroxide than it was before.

"You see what the guy's saying, right?" I said. "I mean, that it's unusual for their government to speak truth, since it's a hotbed of deceit and moral decay; ours, on the other hand, is the soul of integrity."

"Well?" Bud said. "Maybe it's exaggerated, but I don't know how far it is from the truth. I mean, the basic idea."

I looked at Charles. Charles looked back at me. I felt sick, physically sick. I felt fuzzy and light-headed.

"I saw this MTV thing," Charles said. "It was like, about how they're just like us, the people over there, I mean."

"I don't know, Chuck," Bud said. He was done with the peroxide and now he was reading the Neosporin tube.

"Charles has weed work to do out front," I said.

"Hey," Bud said, looking up. "Me and Chuck were getting ready to have a *talk,* you know?"

"Uh-huh," I said. I did an exaggerated turn like a kid playing airplane, arms outstretched. "So the magazine quotes a Russian who said, 'We would like to get our workers to work as hard as your workers.' Now, you figure that's flattery, right? But the magazine plays it for plain fact, since, as the magazine has just said, they tell truth over there now. It's convenient, don't you think?"

Bud was shaking his head like a hundred self-satisfied guys I'd seen on television. He said, "I don't know why you people always want to tear us down."

I wanted to pop his face for him right then, tear it down and drop it into somebody's Night Deposit Box. "Bud," I said, "it's only me here, and I'm not tearing anybody down. This magazine said these people don't work as hard as our people and I say they probably do. They probably work harder. The magazine wants to sell us something, Bud, it wants us to *feel* better, and it's getting us there by saying we work harder—you follow that? It's a pride con— harder equals better; you feel all warm to be an American.

And feeling better is all-important, Bud. If we've got tragic losses along the way, why, it's a small price for national pride; if a few people get killed, well, *maybe they deserve to die.* If we have to splatter and maim like we did for Reagan, so we're tough, so he can pass that along to thousands of small-town papers and hundreds of local nightly news shows, so people interested in breakfast eggs and getting Jim, Jr., through high school can say that they, too, *feel better* about our country, why Bud, that's O.K., cause we were born to rule, right? We were born to minister. That's what *you people* say, isn't it? Born to define. If we only understood what was at stake, we, too, would be willing to forgo a few niceties like law, honesty, justice, fairness, decency, honor—all that, right?"

Bud looked strange. He said, "Well, I wouldn't go that far."

"Hey, Dad," Charles said. "Take it easy on him, will you? Don't bust him up." He patted my shoulder stiffly. "Are you O.K.?"

"Never better," I said, looking at him, feeling how much I liked him, how proud I was that he was my son.

"So, they work as hard as we do, right?" Charles said, trying to get things going again.

Bud was on his feet, capping the peroxide bottle, shuffling gauze pads—he had decided to forgo the Neosporin altogether. "According to your Dad they work harder," he said.

I laughed at him, right at him, to his face, and I didn't feel bad for doing it, though somewhere in my head I was certain that this exchange, like a lot of others I'd had with Bud, would not be forgotten.

"Charles," I said, holding my son but watching Bud, "the Russian guy was being polite and the magazine lied.

The fact is that our workers sit on their butts, smoke cig-arettes, spit, scratch themselves, punch out, and ask for more money. That's the New American Dream. And it goes for all of us, auto unions to university professors."

"Jesus, Peter," Bud said. "I think you're losing per-spective here."

I gave him a big nutsy grin. I was thinking that I sounded just like my father, that Lily was right. My father who complained about everything, bitterly, and at length. He did it at dinner, presumably because there he could be assured an audience; at our house if you wanted to eat you began the meal with the lecture of the day. More often than not that lecture centered on my father's belief that nobody wanted to do anything right. I thought he was nuts—I mean, what was the big deal? How right did you have to do things? And who was to say what was right in the first place? When he talked all I could think of was the other points of view that people might have. His complaints were mostly about people trying to save a buck by cutting corners, and I was always thinking, "Well, maybe there's a good reason to cut a corner or two."

Charles was flapping his shirt. He had it by a button and he was ratcheting the shirt in and out to cool off his chest. I wondered what he was thinking about me.

Bud returned the medicines. "One thing's for sure," he said to Charles. He was using his snide-guy voice. "We're working hard here today. I know your Dad's just back from the Center for Constitutional Studies, but I feel compelled to say that his *opinions* notwithstanding, our people work plenty hard. They earn everything they get."

"Sure," I said. "But earning isn't what it was—if you can pee in a straight line today you can get the big-dollar raise."

"I think you'd better get some sleep," Bud said to me. "You're completely out of control now. You're almost as bad as Lily's brother nowadays."

"Yeah, well, I'm sure Ray would like to discuss this whole issue with you," I said. "While you're at it maybe you can talk fundamental American principles like juicy burgers and jumbo buns."

"Jesus," Bud said. He was trying to find a way to smile politely about that.

"I hate those big fat wet things people always make at home," Charles said. "I'm glad Mom doesn't make those."

At first I didn't get it, but then I figured Charles was supporting me, he was on my side. This was a first, I thought. He was taking on the neighbor, defending the old man, doing a job.

Bud didn't quite get it. "To each his own," he said, limping away from the fence.

I gave him a glazed smile.

Charles said, just loud enough, "Mom makes 'em thin, like Moscow burgers. She does it right. She knows."

Charles and I were silent watching Bud hobble across his yard and into his house. Neither one of us said anything for a minute, and I was standing there staring at the back-yard, which now seemed pleasantly unrestrained, and I had my arm around Charles's shoulder, and I felt O.K. I was thinking that on the one hand I wanted to tell him every-thing, but on the other I'd probably already run him down for the day. What was new was that I didn't feel there was a real rush to get it done. "Your mother makes a good hamburger," I said. "It's not a Whopper, but it's O.K."

Charles laughed, gave me a tight fist and a "Yes" with lots of sibilance, which made me think that I'd said exactly what I was supposed to say at a moment like that, the kind of thing good fathers said. I felt wonderful about that, about doing the right thing, talking to Charles, telling him the truth, and I wanted to cry about that, I felt it coming and I started squinting to slow down the tears. I was thinking that all over America fathers and sons were probably talking just about like we were these days, fathers explaining things, and some of them explaining the same things. And on Monday me and the rest of the old guys would go back to our offices and do the same stuff we always did, and then I realized that what we were really saying, what we were trying to get across to these kids, was that we couldn't do it, that we'd tried, but we couldn't make it. We were telling them that they'd better try.

9 I didn't move to the garage that afternoon, or any of the following afternoons. I didn't even get started. For a couple of weeks things were fine. Ray arrived in town, got an apartment and a job, just as he'd promised Lily he would. He even came by in his new car to introduce his girlfriend, Judy, who looked like she came from money. She was from the Midwest somewhere, small, so small that she was toylike, and she was sexy in an offbeat way. She had wild, stick-up-all-over hair and these eyes that'd cut right through you when she wanted them to—it was like the eyes were talking, the way she looked at you. She was a performer, she said. Actor. Ray told us later she didn't do much of anything.

So in that couple of weeks I spent time with Charles, and with Lily, cleaned up the yard one early evening, watched a TV movie one night, went shopping another night to get Charles a calculator fit for a king, and every night went to bed at a reasonable hour unreasonably content.

Then one morning at two A.M. Lily woke me to tell

me about a dream she'd had. She dreamed of great philosophers, she told me, discussing visions of happiness. There was disagreement among them, apparently, about happiness, and yet there was also agreement.

"This is what happens when great philosophers come together to discuss grave problems," Lily said. "This fissure of views creating the exploitable middle."

I nodded. I wanted to go back to sleep. "Can we talk about this in the morning?"

"C'mon," she said. "At least let me tell you this dream."

So then I got out of bed, went into the kitchen for Diet Coke, came back and sat on the gray-carpeted floor with my back against the bedroom wall. The bedroom was larger than most, so I was farther away than I think she was comfortable with.

She said, "Once upon a time there were three men—" Then she waved. "Really," she said. "In my dream you could tell these three guys were philosophers by the way they looked, bearded, wearing crummy robes with ropes around them, they had tiny sticks in their hair. That's to start with, I mean. They had this look about them, especially their faces."

"That pondering look," I said. "I see a lot of that around the office." I got up off the floor and crawled back into the bed, under the sheets.

"Exactly. They started changing the pants later, one pair on top of another. That was the discussion, the pants. That was the form of the discussion among these guys— bright pants and dark pants, patterned pants."

I was drawing a blank. "I don't get it," I said. "That was the discussion? Changing pants?"

"Crap," she said. "I knew this would happen. It always happens. I have this wonderful dream but when I try to tell somebody about it, somebody doesn't get it. I hate that. I mean, you get something going and all of a sudden *Bang!* somebody doesn't understand it. You're roadblocked in your tracks. Jesus." She sat there a minute, her head twisted a little on her neck, then turned back to me. "Couldn't you just go with this? They talked to each other by changing their pants, that was their way of talking."

"O.K.," I said. "I got it."

Lily folded her legs under her on the bed, sitting alongside me—I was still under the sheets. I gave her some of my Diet Coke, and she took a swallow and said, "Thanks."

"You're welcome," I said. "Now, how did they discuss human happiness with the pants? I believe they did, I just don't quite see how. Even for a dream it's a little, you know, elusive. What did the pants do? Did they do something?"

"The pants sat there on top of the other pants these guys were already wearing. Each pair of pants was an idea of happiness, a complex set of components, notions, ideas, senses, whatnot. That's what it seemed like to me, anyway. One guy would pull on some pants, herringbone maybe, and they would signify something for the other philosophers, who would crane their necks, and scratch their chins, bend this way and that, circle the first guy and study these new slacks. They'd rock to and fro, hold their heads, and that was the way they thought. Just like that."

"Scratching and holding and so on, right?"

"Right," she said. "That was the thinking."

"Uh-huh," I said. "I thought thinking was when you don't say anything for a minute while you let stuff sink in, let it bang around with the other stuff already in your head."

"That's what it used to be," Lily said.

"Oh," I said. I almost called her *Red*, which I'd started to do sometimes as a term of endearment. It was something

I'd picked up from my family; my grandmother used to call my father that, sometimes, or maybe it was my mother who called my father that. Somebody said it, anyway, to my father, who had red hair, when he had hair.

Lily said, "So then one of the two thinking guys would get an idea himself, and *he* would pull on new pants, and the thing'd start again. There was one pair of green pants, real baggy, ballooned, pegged at the bottom with little silver-tipped ankle-belts, but I don't remember which of these guys had 'em. You like green, don't you?"

"Green's what I used to like," I said.

"Well, anyway, I had no idea what the pants meant, you know? So when those guys stopped and studied every new pair I didn't know why. They were just yanking these trousers out of thin air. Bang! Bang! One after another. To me they were just guys in a white space—I mean, they weren't in a room or anything."

"And the pants were their visions of happiness. Do I understand this now?"

"I don't know whether you understand or not," Lily said.

I said, "Were they long pants?"

"What does that matter?" she said. "Yes. They weren't knickers, or whatever you call 'em. They were regular pants like you get at the store. Probably not pants you would buy, or I would buy, but pants you might *see* at the store. Each pair was a hypothesis, a proposition. You know? They were saying things to each other."

"Talking," I said. "What were they saying?"

"They were discussing happiness," she said. "Contrasting views, comparing views, I guess. That kind of thing. Reflecting on happiness, its causes, its allure, its limitations. I don't know. They had all these great pants and that was enough for them. They were like very complex and dense, the pants were, with clues, nuances, shadings. Like logograms or ideograms, or oleographs."

I was sitting in the bed, leaning against the wall behind the bed, with the sheet pulled halfway up my chest, and I had my hands folded across my stomach, which seemed larger than it used to be, and I said, "Lily? Oleographs?"

"I don't know," she said. "Look it up." She was pawing at her hair, forking it with her fingers until it shot straight out from her head. "Anyway, before I fell asleep I was thinking about the No-Pest Strip we need for the flies. They're bad this year; bad in the sense they're always swooping and buzzing when you want them crushed on your rolled-up newspaper." She swatted the air as if taking out flies. "There was a fly here when I was trying to sleep. That's why I was thinking that. Anyway, it's my experience that with the No-Pest Strip you're going to have dead flies all over the floor and you're going to step on them, and so on. I know this because this has happened to me in my lifetime."

"Please stop," I said. "Please."

"I apologize," she said. "There weren't any insects in the dream so I don't know why I'm so interested in them all of a sudden."

"Me neither," I said.

"I should be interested in philosophers. Forget the flies."

"Right," I said.

"These three guys having this extremely pleasing talk with their pants—I wonder if *talk* is the wrong word?"

She looked at the ceiling; I looked, too. Her fly was there, walking in circles on the plasterboard. I saw it but I didn't know if she was looking at it or at something else, so I didn't say anything.

"No," she said, "I think it's right. Talk. The pants were beautiful and every new pair was a deeper pleasure than the last. One pair had moonbeams. Jesus, they went for the moonbeams. Blue slats of moonlight with giraffes in them. African, I think the giraffes were." She seemed suddenly to pull away from me, to close down our talk, to become distant and wrapped in her own thought. "The giraffes had these drums strapped to their sides—looked like conga drums, but they might have been tom-toms."

"I said, "Wait a minute, Lily, is this a real dream or are you just making this dream up as you go along?"

"It's real," she said. "I dreamed it myself."

I said, "If these guys put the pants on one on top of another—"

"I know what you're thinking," she said. "They got real bulky. But that was part of the idea, maybe. One guy was remarkably bulky when I woke up. The philosophers were happy, though, you could see that."

"What about you?"

She screwed up her face and flipped her hand as if telling me to get out of the bed, to get across the room. "No, they were over there. I was just watching. I don't know what I felt. I felt asleep, I guess. I wasn't in the dream, I was just dreaming it. It was their dream."

That stopped the talk for a minute and I heard a car passing by out in the street, rolling by real slow, the engine throttled way back, almost at idle, but still loud, thumping. Maybe that thumping was the car radio. Some rap tune. The glass in our bedroom window chattered a minute and I was suddenly aware of other things—a bird somewhere, an airplane coming or going, tired-looking street lamps outside wrapped in tired-looking light, the wind jerking around.

Then Lily said, "They were naked except for these pants."

"You said they were wearing robes."

"I lied about that. I was afraid you'd get upset."

Someplace outside there was a crack, a backfire or a gun blast. A spider went across the ceiling. I said, "So these philosopher guys were, like, nude from the waist up?"

"No," she said. "They were totally nude. *Hugely* nude. But they were dealing with pretty tricky questions, and the pants were going on and coming off so fast that you didn't see all that much, really. And maybe the talk wasn't just what the pants *looked* like, but also stuff like how they fit, and fabrics and dyes, you know?, cuts and weaves, pockets, welts . . . All that counted. And besides, these guys were *enchanted*. They were there with their big thick beards, and their fluttering beautiful pale-colored pants, and they looked like they were just back from the Middle Ages and ancient times."

"Nude," I said.

"Well . . . yeah," she said.

Then the air conditioner snapped on and she halted a minute, staring up at the register high on the wall. "There wasn't any fruit in the dream," she said. "I associate fruit with happiness, so I expected fruit, maybe fruit patterns, fruit colors, but there wasn't any of that."

"Sun's coming up," I said, pointing at the dark window.

"No, I mean it," she said. "You could really discuss the hell out of happiness if you had fruit. But there wasn't any in the dream. I think that was a serious flaw."

I said, "Well, that's one of the risks, isn't it? When you go to bed. When you sleep. When you dream."

"What's a risk?" Lily said. "What do you mean?"

"That you miss stuff," I said.

"You mean that things go wrong, sometimes?"

"Yeah. Things go wrong in your dreams," I said.

"Oh," she said.

Then we smiled at each other an odd smile, not really unfriendly, but cagey, one that knew a lot of stuff about both of us, a lot of what had happened, and a lot of what was to happen.

"I like mine anyway," she said.

"What *was* yours, exactly?" I said. "What did the guys decide?"

"That there is the possibility of good fortune," she said.

She gave me a look then, one of her looks, her hair pulled out wild and her eyes telling me all kinds of crazy things.

It was a clean look, full of recognition and understanding, loaded with what goes on between people who care for each other. It wasn't even a surprise, really, but there it was and we enjoyed it. After that we were rustling around in the sheets, getting settled, smoothing covers and breathing a lot more carefully than we had been; it seemed as if we were just glancing off into the middle distance together. It seemed like we saw the future.

10 The house I leased was a ranch-style brick three bedroom in an early-sixties subdivision called Rolling Hills, a place not at all unlike the one we'd started in years before, her house, except in my case there was an apartment project across the street. My house had high horizontal windows in the bedrooms, fake parquet floors, four-by-four tile in the bathrooms and the kitchen. It had a low two-car garage with lots of thorny bushes around it, a backyard the size of an extra two-car garage, and four-foot metal fencing all around.

I wasn't sure why the move was necessary, or even that it was. My sense has always been that things happen for complicated reasons and that when we try to figure out why we've done what we've done, we don't get very close, but we get tired, so we stop figuring. This wasn't any different. I had no goal except to be more easygoing, to let stuff roll off my back more readily; in the meantime I was going private. This seemed reasonable—maybe if I had no one to complain to that'd slow me down. Moving was something I could do, anyway, to signal myself that I was trying to do something. Lily said I didn't complain as much as I thought, and I told her that I never thought of anything but complaints, that stuff was always screaming through my head. I hoped I'd feel better if I got away.

It'd always been curious to listen to people at the office when they talked about their lives—everything sounded so simple. These were lives thick with cause and effect; nobody ever did anything that wasn't understood right down to the shoe leather. These people could explain everything they did in the clearest, most coherent detail—"because of this I did that, and then that happened, so I did this"—it was all precise and direct and sensible and sturdy. Nothing like the way we lived.

"People always do this kind of thing, don't they?" she'd said the night of her dream. "Does it ever do any good? Doesn't it just make more trouble?"

"I don't know," I said. "I've never done it before."

"I want you to feel better," she said.

"Me, too," I said. "And I ought to. I don't know why I don't. I mean what would Jesus do in my shoes?"

"He probably wouldn't compare himself to Jesus if he were in your shoes."

"He wouldn't have to, would he?" I said. "But I get the point."

"So you're moving because you hate everything, is that why?" she asked. There were tears in her eyes, tiny crystals, like sudden glints caught on a leaf in a forest; I thought I'd probably never love anybody as much as I loved her right then, as much as I had always loved her. I held her, wrapped her up and tightened down around her arms, felt the fear in her shoulders, smelled her hair.

In a minute I gave her a final squeeze and said, "You're probably the last interesting woman in the country. Meanwhile, it was O.K. out there when it was *Masterpiece Theatre* and edgy Italian movies, French movies, but now the brain-sluts have taken over and I'm going to go berserk. I need to take a breather."

"So, Peter, is this a good reason for you to leave?"

"I don't know. Probably not. But I'm getting another place. I won't have to feel bad around here."

"Right," she said, sternly. Then she unknotted her face. "I don't mean to be making fun, O.K.? I understand that this is serious. I just want you to stay close. I don't want you never coming back."

.   .   .

So I leased this house ten miles from Lily, and on the day I moved Ray and Judy helped me shift things over, clothes mostly, because the house was furnished, and that was that. For the first month I slept in the new place but went by Lily's often, sometimes for meals, sometimes to take her and Charles to the mall, sometimes for no reason, so the three of us saw a lot of each other. It was refreshing seeing them in this new way. Our life felt different—Lily and I seemed like two separate people, which was interesting and energizing. I thought Charles and I ought to spend time alone together, so I started inviting him to stay more with me. Sometimes he'd come for one night, sometimes for weekends.

One Saturday night Charles told me he wanted to learn to drive. It was silly, but when I was talking to Lily later that night and I brought it up she insisted that Charles ought to be humored in this, and that I should do the humoring. "It's such a father and son thing," she said to me on the telephone.

Charles became precious, suddenly. In a short time I

moved past infatuation and headed for obsession. I talked
to Lily about this all the time. I asked her questions about
him, about what he did and how he did it, about his school,
and his hobbies, and I asked about the way he acted with
her so I could compare it with the way he acted with me.
There was no sign that Charles returned my interest, and
that accounted in part, perhaps, for the intensity of my
feeling. I started thinking of MY SON all the time, in capital
letters, in the middles of meetings, at dinners with clients.
I wondered what Charles was doing at particular moments
of the day, wondered where he was, what he was thinking.
I felt disabled at times like these, dazed by what I didn't
know about him, by how distant and unconnected I felt, as
if Charles were a kid in a television commercial, a kid de-
signed to be distant.

One of the things that had gone on recently, both
before I moved and after, was that I didn't like to imagine
being without him. There was something between us.

I told Lily, "It's not that we share so much or any of
that crap, but we're father and son. We don't have much
time, we don't have much in common, but, Jesus, I love to
look at him, I feel like a teenager. I like the way he watches
me back while he's pretending he's watching TV shows."

"I know," she said. "I see it. He talks about you back
here. He thinks you're wonderful, but he thinks you're crazy,
too. You know, you ought to just leave him alone sometimes. Let him get there on his own hook."

"Everything's delicate," I said. "It's too bad you have
to get this far away to see it. I'm even afraid that after a
while Charles and I will blur back to etiquette."

"Well, don't worry about it," she said. "If you're worrying about that you're already worrying too much, you're
worrying about something that will never happen."

I started wanting a child when I began to think how lonely I was going to be when I got old. This was after Charles was born, when he was two or three. Everybody else in my old folks' home was going to have these people visiting and I was going to be sitting there with the people that time forgot. For a while I thought that was a real selfish idea and I didn't want to admit I was having a child just so somebody would be around to come and see me when I was seventy. And I was counting on that, that coming around, even though I knew it wasn't commonplace anymore, it wasn't the way things happened.

Later I figured that my situation with Charles was only typical. I imagined myself forty years into the future on a porch in too-big mail-order trousers, and I imagined Charles lumbering up the walk, big artificial smile on his face, or maybe some grim look, if we'd progressed to the gritty-is-genuine stage. I imagined the two of us arguing, Charles getting after me for being stubborn about my hearing, or for being unwilling to do something he wanted done. When Lily and I married, and when she got pregnant, I didn't figure on this odd business of the living annuity. But I figured on it now, felt it; I was afraid of the future just like the next guy, the future as it honed in tight, raised its welts. My real worry about spending time away from Lily wasn't that I loved her so much that I couldn't stand to be without her now—I loved her, but I could stand it—but that we wouldn't have a chance to be together later, in the future when magazine-love wasn't on anyone's mind, when the fear of everybody else had vanished, been outlived, and the love we had would be something calmer, quieter, richer than what was advertised.

So we had Charles, a walking, talking insurance policy, an ounce of prevention, an edge against what wasn't known, what was out there, whatever mayhem awaited. Charles would call us and cater to us and kiss us awkwardly in our old age. Charles would come on weekends. Charles would want to argue and would want to introduce us to his women friends, to his wife, finally to his children. More children. Charles was something for us to do in the future, was our future; he was for that time when what we thought was important wasn't important anymore.

.   .   .

For Charles's dinner I baked chicken breasts and put a pack of frozen peas in a pan and did a potato wrapped in a napkin in the microwave. All this I served on paper plates at the eating bar that was one of the walls of my kitchen. I was sort of proud of this food because it looked so much like a regular meal, plates notwithstanding. I'd even set the eating bar with place mats, napkins, a full service of knives and forks, salt and pepper in these odd, cow-shaped shakers I'd picked up at the grocery—the works. When we sat down to eat Charles told me he wanted to practice driving in the morning, if that was O.K.

I said, "There's no reason in the world you should be driving at your age, Charles."

"I know," he said. "But I need to learn."

"What for?"

"I want to be ready to go at fourteen," Charles said.

"Fourteen?" I said.

"Sure," he said. "Learner's, anyway."

After dinner we sat together in the living room with the TV on. We had our feet up, all four of them. Charles liked television, MTV mostly, but he already loved to change the channels. Bang!—he went through them faster than I did. This struck me as both funny and touching, and then I realized that I hadn't done all that badly with Charles, that *we* hadn't.

"I'll tell you what," I said. "In the morning maybe we can go out to the Wal-Mart, something like that, maybe buy a *radio-controlled* car, huh? How would that be?"

"That'd be great, Dad," Charles said, but I could tell from the look on his face it was a big letdown.

"Well, you know," I said, "radio control is a good place to start. I mean, practice your steering, application of brakes—you know. It's pretty much the real thing, isn't it?"

"That's great, Dad," he said.

"Well," I said. "It's smaller, maybe. But . . ."

·   ·   ·

On Sunday morning in the parking lot outside the new Wal-Mart I felt thoroughly connected to the world around me, just like every other middle-aged male, married twice, divorced once, having trouble with the second one; I felt especially connected as I waited in the front seat of my car for Charles to emerge from the store with whatever radio-controlled toy had struck his fancy. At home just before ten that morning I had wondered aloud if we might be better off forgetting the whole project. Then Charles had said to me that I "always argued against everything." I thought, and said, that was an exaggeration, but on that Sunday morning across the stained Formica cabinet-top the comment had a remarkable impact. I stopped arguing, pulled on my sweatshirt with TIME HAS NO MEANING printed on the front, swept car keys and wallet off the counter, grabbed Charles's arm, and headed out the door.

And now I was sitting in the parking lot outside Wal-

Mart, in the first space next to the handicapped space, waiting for Charles to emerge, watching an extremely fat woman in a jumpsuit, a pink exercise jumpsuit, a woman so fat that she looked as if she needed legs to hold up her legs, watching her navigate the distance between her chrome-yellow high-rise pickup truck and the entrance of the store.

I shook my head and wheezed, "Hail Mary, full of grace."

This spontaneous expression of opinion made me feel bad because I had no right to judge the woman, because I should have had more compassion. She didn't like being a pig of a woman any more than I liked looking at her and seeing that she was a pig of a woman. I should have just looked the other way. But I couldn't because the woman wobbled like a fat collector, like she was a home for wayward fat, a fat magnet.

I wondered if she had a disease, a thyroid condition that produced fat at such an extraordinary rate that it could not be contained. That it flew out of her system, thickening the air around her. If not that, what? What other explanation might there be? I looked at her shoes, low white pumps her feet overflowed; these shoes had small heels on them. They looked startled by what they were asked to carry. Why didn't a doctor help her? Why didn't some fire department help her?

I felt guilty for a second, and then I figured she was just some fleshy swine glutton sack of gland meat barely able to struggle out of her own slop long enough to buy her favorite Grotesque & Lurid four-by-four tunic at Wal-Mart, barely able to stretch it enough to get it around her face, much less the rest of her, so I quit worrying and started watching a guy spraying the side of the brick building with a hose. The man was squirting the hose in a pattern, writing letters with the water stream, then erasing what he'd written almost immediately by scratching it out with the stream. The words only stayed up a few seconds, and the water barely darkened the brick, so his scribblings were hard to read. He wrote what looked like the word *illegal,* and then the word *honey*-something, I couldn't make out what. It seemed to me it had to be honeypie, or honeypot.

I was watching this man, who had on a T-shirt two sizes too small in spite of the weather, which was cool, when there was a knock on my car window. I turned in the seat to look and then I had to jump back because a girl's face was very close to the glass, almost pressed against it, and for a moment I even thought I could see the image of her eye makeup smudged there on the window. She made a feverish circling gesture with her right hand, telling me to roll down my window, not realizing, apparently, that the car windows were electric. I waved at her with my right hand and then reached around the steering wheel to turn the key so as to get electricity to roll down the window. At the same time, I was reaching with my left hand for the window roller-downer switch.

The first thing I heard after the suction of the window backing down and out of its trace was the girl's voice. She said, "I guess I've been out here for an hour or something, it's crazy, I've been standing right here by your car, what are you doing?"

"I'm sorry?" I said.

"I'm not at all certain sorry is going to get it, chum," the girl said. Her face was pressed right up into the window frame, eight inches away from mine.

"I think we have a mistake," I said. "My name is Peter Wexler. I'm waiting for my son, Charles, who's in the Wal-Mart there buying a radio-controlled car."

"Well, that's charming," the girl said. "We're introducing ourselves, now. My name's Gayla. You've been assigned to me."

"Gayla?" I said.

"Yeah," the girl said. "You know, like the kites." She backed up and waved her hand toward the sky. "This is my end of the parking lot, and I'm assigned everybody who comes into it. You're my customer."

"Well, how can I help you?" I said. When the girl backed away from the car I could see that she was quite attractive under all the makeup and the thin chains and the witty clothes. Maybe she was twelve, maybe fourteen. She had clean soapy skin, almost white hair, and she seemed as thin under her clothes as a crease in a tablecloth.

"You can start by giving me twelve-fifty," the girl said. "Or twenty-two dollars for the Bonus Pack."

"The Bonus Pack?" I said.

"Peanut brittle," the girl said. She held up a sack that she had been carrying, a small shopping bag from a ritzy department store with another bag inside it. She shook the two bags. I heard nothing. "Peanut brittle," she repeated.

"Good idea," I said, twisting over in the seat so that I could reach my wallet in my left rear pants pocket. "Hang on a minute."

"My name's Gayla," the girl said. Seeing that I was reaching for my wallet, she had finally decided to shake hands with me.

Just then I saw Charles coming out of the store. He was reading a box that he was carrying, a large box, a colorful box. He was intent on what he was reading. He was sort of wandering in our direction.

I took the girl's hand and shook it quickly. I said, "I'm

Peter. And that's Charles, my son, coming at us there." I pointed to Charles.

Gayla turned around and looked over her shoulder.

I said, "I don't have any change. Can you take a check?" I wagged my checkbook out the car window.

Gayla sighed and shook her head, looking pointedly at the blacktop. Then she shrugged. "Sure," she said. "Knock yourself out."

I started making out the check.

There was an odd scene when Charles got to the car. He got in on his side and then he and this girl stared at each other for a minute. Glowered at each other. She was standing right by my window looking in; he was sitting in the passenger seat with his body facing forward but his head snapped around toward her.

"Hi," he said.

She just waved at him.

I ripped off the check and handed it to her, and she handed me two plastic bags of peanut brittle.

"Thanks," I said.

"Think nothing of it," she said.

.   .   .

When we got back on the freeway I said, "Who was that?" He had been reading his box since the business with Gayla, and he had just finished reading and put the box back into its bag. He'd bought some kind of truck, it looked like.

"I know her from school, you know? She's ultra-weird. She's the one who tried to kill herself or something, or that's what they say, anyway. I don't really believe it."

"Oh yeah?" I said, taking a look toward the Wal-Mart parking lot. I turned back to Charles. "I think we ought to get something straight. I'm not sure I'm going to be interested in radio control anymore."

"You suggested it," he said.

"I know I did, but I realized when you were inside there that I'm not as interested as I thought I was. I guess that makes me a bad dad, huh?"

"No, that's all right, Dad," Charles said. "I *like* to do things alone. I like this." He tapped the box. "Off-road," he said.

I said, "I was interested when I ordered all that stuff from California? All those cars?"

"Yeah," Charles said. "I remember. But those were for you. Those weren't for me."

"They could have been for you," I said.

"Sure, after you were done with them," Charles said.

"We could have played with them together," I said. "I mean, I may have been stingy at first, but—"

Charles picked up one of the two bags of peanut brittle. "That's O.K., Dad," he said, holding the bag between his thumb and forefinger. He spun it. "I've got my stuff and you've got your stuff. That's the way it is. That's the way it's supposed to be, isn't it?"

"I guess so," I said. "I don't know, really, how it's supposed to be, I mean. I don't think anybody knows how it's supposed to be. You know what I mean? I mean, it's just a certain way, and that's how it's supposed to be. Between fathers and sons, I mean."

"Yeah," Charles said. "That's what they say on TV."

We drove the rest of the way to the house in silence; I was watching the road, watching the trees along the side of the road, watching the women in the cars on the road. Charles thumped his thumb against his box and stared straight out the front window. When we got into the driveway, just short of the garage, I knocked the gear-lever up into Park and turned off the key. There was a minute then when we were sitting in the car together with the engine off, neither of us making an effort to get out, and it was a stinging moment, full of portent, full of stuff that was supposed to be said but wasn't getting said, full of the difficulty of just going on, just getting yourself on to the next thing. After a minute I turned and saw that Charles was sitting there wiping his eyes, really going after them, rubbing and wiping and rubbing again, like he was crying but trying to cover it up.

I said, "You must be a pretty lonely guy, huh, Charles?"

He gave me an adult look like *What are you talking about?* then grinned and reached to touch my shoulder, to give me a pat. "No," he said. "Not really. I'm fine. Why'd you say that? Are you O.K.? Are you upset about this stuff with the car? Or something else? That girl I was telling you about? Are you feeling guilty? You could probably get up some enthusiasm if you had to, couldn't you? For the cars?"

"Sure," I said.

He grinned at me. "I'm really O.K., Dad," he said. "I just feel bad. I think I may be carsick. Didn't I used to get carsick all the time? When I was a kid?"

.   .   .

When we first bought a house I thought I was going to be O.K. about it, I thought I wasn't going to feel constrained or anything, and that it was just another step in a series of steps in a reasonably choreographed life—not too much, not too little. Now, in the driveway outside my rented brick house, I thought it was stupid to blame the house for the way I felt, it was stupid to blame anybody for anything. It was stupid to take as my own personal responsibility the protection of all Americans everywhere from the raging in-justices and untruths that they were themselves actively engaged in, it was stupid to think that the world was going to suddenly turn better the way weather does in the fall of every year when suddenly all the pressure disappears and everything is possible again because it's not so hot as it was, it's cool, even, there's a breeze, and there's the scent of Halloween and Thanksgiving and Christmas blowing through the trees, rustling the leaves, sweeping away the fallen, tracing the light blue sky with quick thin clouds and suggestions of better days to come, of sweeter smells and softer nights and of rain that barely falls. Rain that sifts down so scarcely that it can hardly be known without feeling it on your cheeks. Stupid and lovely. So I was thinking these things, I was realizing these things while I sat in the driver's seat of the car, my feet out on the concrete drive, while I bent over for a second, putting my head in my hands, my palms covering my eyes, and listened to Charles's footsteps heading into the garage.

· · ·

Charles had the new radio-control monster truck up and running. It hadn't required much preparation. The truck was a four-by-four called "The Invalidator," a foot or more long and about a foot high—one-quarter-inch scale, the box said; it was the size of a small dog, and it had fat air-filled tractor-style tires, and it was trimmed and decaled and striped and flamed and chromed to within an inch of its overbright plastic life. It was a lot fancier than the kits I'd ordered from California.

I watched my son ram the killer truck into the legs of furniture, forward, then backward, in skittering circles and in bumpy and tilting straight lines on long runs across the room, head-on into the baseboard.

"Yes, Charles," I finally said.

"Huh? Yes what?" Charles was crouched alongside the sofa doctoring the truck's plastic nerf bar.

"Carsick," I said. "You used to be carsick all the time. After a while we thought you were faking it." I made a face and apologized all in one motion. "You want to help me write a suicide note?"

"Huh?" Charles said. He gave me a look and then said, "Why don't you write it and read it to me later, O.K.?"

"Well, what do you think it ought to say?"

"Make it gruesome," he said.

It should be an indictment of all the wrong stuff, the litany of dread and distaste, imprecise reason, unfocused anger, domestic frustration, powerlessness, disenfranchisement, personal shortfall, rejection, weakness and guilt, self-indulgence, boredom, physical decline, self-loathing, and so on and on, all comprising reasons I was sitting in a rented house with a nice kid and a brand-new, charmingly belligerent, radio-control truck.

"I was thinking we could do it together," I said. I sat on a stool in the kitchen, in the door between the kitchen and the den, and got a yellow pad ready. I was staring at my reflection in the sliding door of the den. "How about if it starts 'To Whom It May Concern,' " I said. "How's that?"

"Oh *sure*, Dad," Charles said. "It's old Mr. Dweeb-oid. Hey, it's *supposed* to be scary. You're not even close. Blood squirting out, you know? Skin ripped off, fingers baked, eyeballs exploding—get some slime going in there. Slime yourself to death. Give me some blistering electroshock burning-hair spurting membrane—you know what I'm saying?"

I nodded at all that. That made sense to me. I said, "How about, 'I loathe, abominate, revile, and scorn—' "

"No, no, no . . ." he said, holding his head in his hands.

"Wait," I said. "How about 'I want to puke glistening curly strings of bloody slime-coated intestine into the dainty white face of everyday life.' "

"Hey!" Charles said. "Way to go, Dad. Way to start." He was going down the hall, toward his room, the room I'd fixed for him. "Hey, Dad?" he shouted from down there. He was out of sight. "Can I get Taco-Bell later?"

.   .   .

It was about three in the morning when I got out of bed and put on my jeans, went through the house to Charles's room to see if Charles was sleeping. He was. It was raining. The truck was on the floor by the bed. The tires were on the table that I had made for him out of sawhorses and a hollow-core door, a family tradition. I stood in the room a minute and watched Charles sleep, then I went through the house into the kitchen, got a Diet Coke, went outside, and got into my car, which was still parked in the driveway, in the rain, the water spattering off the windshield, off the hood, beating on the roof. The streetlights, one right across the street from my house and several down the street, were haloed like the lights on every spacecraft since *Close Encounters*. It was the middle of the night and nobody was out. I looked at the line of cars in front of the apartments across from my house. I counted four BMWs, a Mercedes, two Volvos, several Hondas, and a number of the newer American cars, the ones that were rounded off and shaped like nineties versions of fifties streamliners. There was a lot of rain, pretty rain, and I sat in the car and watched it.

I used to sit out in the car at night all the time before I married Lily. After we were married we did it together for a while. Then it tailed off. I'd started again when I moved. The car was comfortable, close, and being in it was restful. I knew all its odd smells, its creaks, knew its shapes in the dark. And I liked the closeness of things, that it was small and tight and focused and fitted. Three hundred sixty degrees of glass. It was like a submarine, or an attack vehicle, or an instrument of science, or a weapon inside of which I was fully protected. Looking at the apartments across the street I remembered how we used to know our neighbors, Lily and me, not well, not to have over to dinner, but to say hello to, to exchange pleasantries with in a store parking lot, or to wave at from the door or the driveway. But the people now, in this new place, on my side of the street and across the street, I didn't seem to know them all that well.

I was startled by Charles cracking on the glass. I opened the door and said, "Hey, what are you doing? You were asleep, weren't you?"

"Let me in," he said, pushing my shoulder.

I moved, looping my legs over the gear lever, settling into the passenger seat and leaving the driver's side for him. I said, "Are you wet?"

"No, Dad," he said, rolling his eyes. "Not much. Why are you sitting out here?"

"I don't know. Tired, I guess."

"Yeah. Me too," he said.

I was suddenly glad the son I had was Charles and not some other kid. Charles could fend for himself, he was tough, and he was forgiving. I could make mistakes, and

11 Charles got a special award as the most mathematical fifth-grader so I went to his school one night, to a PTA meeting. At the reception after the ceremony I headed for the punch, even though the punch table was surrounded on three sides by earnest-looking parents—clean, bright faces, ready smiles, the knowing and glowing types who measure quality of mind in terms of violence to the dress code. I was thinking it must be generational, this tendency to wear gym shorts and an Armani jacket. I liked the look. When I got around behind the table I stepped over a brick planter and tripped, banging into the woman who was serving. Punch went flying. Most of it hit the floor, but there was some on me, some on her. She patted at her clothes and introduced herself. "I'm Maria Shing. I teach here—eighth grade, civics." She scanned the crowd as she dried. There were a hundred very modern people there, among the tan folding chairs. "I hate these things, don't you?" she said.

"I don't come very often," I said. "I'm Peter Wexler, Charles's father."

"Do I know Charles?" she said.

"He's there," I said, pointing him out in a small crowd of kids by the back door. "He won fifth-grade math."

"Oh," she said. "Congratulations. And no, I don't know him. He's too young for me." Then, looking around more, she said, "Take a look at this bean pole over here." She was showing me a guy who was basketball-player tall. "Sixth grade."

"Uh-huh," I said. I liked it that she called him a bean pole. I handed a woman who had come for punch a couple of blood-red napkins. That became my job, the napkins. I handed them out while Maria ladled. We spent an hour doing that and talking about divorces—the separation from Lily didn't qualify, but I had the first divorce to fall back on. It was a good hour, funny and hopeful, the kind of thing that happens out of nowhere and makes you think things are possible again. When the reception thinned I collected Charles and the three of us walked out together.

Maria started to fluff Charles's hair when I introduced them, but thought better of it and stopped mid-gesture. "You don't look like a Charles," she said. "You look like a Lance, or a Marsh."

"What's a Lance look like?" Charles said.

We stopped between two lines of cars in the parking lot and I put my arm around Charles and said, "I think he's more of a Mick. He's got a Mick look about him."

"What are you guys talking about?" Charles said. "Dad, can we go to the mall? I think I want to get a hamster. Can I have a hamster?"

"If you eat it when you get tired of it," I said. Ordinarily, Charles would have come with his mother, but Lily had a business dinner, so I got an extra night.

"Sometimes he actually calls me Charles," Charles said.

He was towing me toward the car. "Can we roll outta here?"

"Sure," I said.

Maria held out her hand. "Well, it was nice to meet you. The ones I usually meet are either crazy for parenthood or hot for drama, which means anything that happens while they're horizontal."

"Thanks," I said. "I think."

"That's right," she said. "People can't stand the day-to-day, and after a while that's all I care about, that's where you make or break."

I took the hand she offered and held it longer than necessary, in more ways than necessary, imagining her for a minute or two—her nights, her habits, her privacy. Finally I said, "I guess day-to-day is my middle name."

A teenage girl went by in jeans and an Ocean Pacific shirt. "Yo, Charles," she said. "What's doing? You get your permit?"

"Isn't that what's-her-name?" I said.

"Yep," he said.

"She looks different," I said.

On the way home I pumped him for what he knew about Maria Shing. Charles was uncooperative. He didn't know a thing. He said, "You want me to ask about her?"

"No. I don't know," I said. "I just wondered."

"I could go around to all my friends and tell them my dad flipped out for Miss Shing and ask them what she's like."

"No, thanks," I said. "Let's change the subject. I'm sorry I brought it up."

We stopped at a light bracketed on four corners by three different fried chicken franchises and one burger joint. Charles said, "Do you like her a lot? I guess she's probably going to be your girlfriend now. You guys'll get married and everything. If that's what's happening I'm telling Mom."

"Go easy on me, Charles," I said. "I'm a casualty."

"Oh, Dad," he said, slapping at my leg. "What's that mean? Why do you always say things I don't understand?"

I pulled him over next to me in the seat, sat with my arm around his small shoulders as if he were six again, as if it were years ago. He leaned his head against my chest.

"That's the way it goes," I said. "When you get old like me you get to be a mystery. It'll happen to you quick enough."

"I don't want to be a mystery," Charles said. "I never want to be a mystery."

12 I went to Birmingham to visit the company I'd found to finish assembly of the tiny wind-up apes an ad agency had sold its client as part of an ape concept promotion. That was before the agency discovered it couldn't get a suitable ape to save its soul. They had a real estate client and a "we're going ape over you" promotion. Visiting the plant was a goodwill gesture for us, because the deal looked like it needed that. We were into these people for thirty-five thousand tiny red wind-up apes, three-inch apes, and we thought the guy on the other end could use a pat on the back. So I'd gone over to nod at the production line, to get impressed, and to make sure they could supply the apes on time and under budget, as if we cared, finally. But we said it sincerely, endlessly, the prescription part of our dress code.

It was crazy, but the jokers at the office were proud of me for finding these apes. It was a breakthrough, money in the bank, people delighted about the fine job with the wind-ups. We'd done a morning performance, me and the agency guy, Bob Moserine, and then somebody's idea of a brunch, coffee and shrink-wrapped cake doughnuts, and then we'd had lunch with five sincerely ugly men and one lonely woman, then we had an afternoon tour of the plant, then a meeting, and finally, at six-thirty I was back at the Ramada trying to get rid of the grime when a woman came to the door. She gave a quick knock and just walked right in when I opened up. I was bundled in a towel. I'd been at the other end of the room, at the lav, working on my teeth. I'd been very diligent about my teeth since the dentist told me I was losing the war and gave me the *National Enquirer* version of periodontics—a graphic story of how teeth separate from bone, how plaque eats bone, how teeth skate and prowl and twitch themselves right out of your mouth given half a chance.

The woman said, "Hi," only she made it a question, more tentative than I'd expected from somebody walking into somebody else's motel room, and I didn't know what to make of it. The woman had that plain-faced modern look—decent features but nothing much dramatic except this thing around the eyes, the way she looked at you as if she meant business, she'd do anything, and she'd enjoy doing it. I took about ten seconds to go through the woman-walks-into-your-motel-room fantasy, the good-looking woman with long legs, a ruthless dress, and evil in her eyes. Just about like this one. Then I said, "Excuse me? Are you with Bloodman?"

Bloodman was the ape company—I thought she might be somebody coming to advise me of a change of plans, dinner on the grass out back of the parking lot or something like that. Something to make my day more charming than it had already been.

"Yes," she said. "My name is Dorothy."

"Great," I said. Then I figured she must have been Paul

Warner's idea of a successful visit joke. Paul Warner was our contact at Bloodman, their hotshot sales guy. He liked to call himself Numero Uno in a self-effacing way so that it looked as if he was making fun of his success when he was, in fact, bragging about it. He made everybody at the company sick. Everybody.

She stepped sideways into the room, skirting the bed. "I thought I'd come by, you know, after everything was over, to see how you were. I thought maybe you'd be ready for a quiet dinner or something. My name's Dorothy?"

It was another question, as if I was supposed to know. "You said that," I said, hooking my left thumb into the waist of the towel I had on to be sure it stayed put. I extended a hand. "Peter Wexler," I said. "Hello, Dorothy." I waved toward the leatherette chair in the corner. "Take a seat. Let me get something on."

"Go ahead," she said. "We've got plenty of time." She swiveled and stepped for the chair, bending at the waist and knee to slide past the table. "You don't remember me, do you?"

I grabbed a pair of jeans off the television set and headed for the bathroom. "Is this a joke? Paul's idea of a joke? Is it a setup? I don't mean to be rude."

"Don't worry," she said. I thought I heard her whistling, just barely, just something a shade above a hiss. Then she said, "Ray's ex, remember?"

I was stepping into the pants behind the half-closed bathroom door, having trouble with my leg, the wet skin sticking, catching in the pants leg. Who she was snapped into my brain—we'd met once, years ago, on one of Ray's revisit-the-home-county expeditions. She had come sometime before the parrot woman and before he went into the water business, and it had been a short marriage, probably unfortunate for her. I'd liked her then, everybody had liked her except Ray. "How are you?" I said, leaning so I was speaking out between the edge of the door and the jamb.

"I talked to Ray," she said. "That's how I knew. And the ape order is hot, too. Normally, if somebody wants that many they go straight to Taiwan. We don't even get a piece of it."

When I was dressed we went out: Her car was an old Chevrolet, a late-fifties job that looked as if somebody had worked long and hard to bring it back up to spec. I asked and she told me the Chevy had been in her family all along, that her mother had bought it brand-new in 1958 and had died shortly thereafter, leaving the almost undriven car in the garage with four-foot walls her father had built as a reaction to an article he'd read about the A-bomb in *Life*. "It was airtight," she said. "We had our own special air system, Dad did, I mean. But it was really ours, since we spent a lot of time playing out there. It was like our play-room, and all the time there was the Chevy in it, all covered up with cheesecloth or something, a weird fabric he bought mail order that was supposed to retard the effects of radia-tion on the paint. He was a stickler for good paint. He always said that if GM had gone to decent paints it could jump the prices on its cars twelve, maybe fifteen percent. He said people would pay for quality. He always said that."

"I guess it's true, too," I said.

"If they recognize it," Dorothy said. "Usually they have about as much chance as a cat in a gas fire. But I like the car. It's only got six thousand miles," she said. "It might as well be yesterday. You still with Lily?"

"Yes," I said. I said it quickly, without thinking, which left me in the awkward position of trying to explain. "We're not living together right now. You know, that kind of thing."

"There's a lot of that," she said. "But people are getting tired of it. There's less than before."

"So I'm told. I think it's just that we don't want to hear about it anymore, we figure it's dead-end stuff. People get together, fall apart, get back together—it never ends. There's nothing to learn, no changing it. It makes everybody tired."

"You believe that?"

"No," I said. "Sometimes."

. . .

We were driving through late-evening light that was shadowy and thick, like lines of bright glass slanting down hard between two threads of dark tall pines on this old highway. We'd already clicked on our lights. Dorothy told me a story about a friend of hers who'd been knocked off a huge bridge over the Mississippi River at Baton Rouge. The bridge was all steel, girders and lacy mesh, maybe a hundred and fifty feet over the water at its highest point, and in a freak thing a guy running a crane that was being used to repair the guardrail on one side of the bridge zigged when he was supposed to zag and knocked the woman's yellow Pinto off the overpass. Her car fell the hundred and fifty feet nose first into the river, hit it like a giant bullet and jammed into the mud bottom like an underwater Louisiana version of the famous West Texas car sculpture.

It was a grotesque story, and I kept saying "C'mon, are you sure?"

She kept saying she was.

So she had the car and she was doing the driving and after about twenty minutes on a couple of highways that didn't seem much used she said, "I can be quiet if you prefer."

I said, "I was thinking it would be nice to stop somewhere."

"O.K.," Dorothy said, staring ahead, out the windshield where the highway was now lit mostly by her headlights and the occasional brights of passing trucks. She didn't say anything for a few minutes, she just drove, quiet, like saying something wasn't even in her universe. Finally she said, "What? You want me to pull over somewhere through here where the bushes are especially thick and the crickets especially vigorous and get the thing done? That'd be pretty interesting, wouldn't it? Just you and me here in the backseat of this Chevy four-door hardtop, just the way it was supposed to be back then, but wasn't? Me sweet and proper and you at once too eager and too unschooled to get the job done cleanly? That's the nature of the deal, isn't it? The way it went or the way it was supposed to have gone, even if it didn't go that way at all, even if one or the other of us had to wait a few years beyond the expected on an aluminum chaise on somebody's porch in the middle of a summer heat wave so that the skin stuck like glazer's cups—"

I said. "Sorry. I didn't mean that. I just don't remember you very well and it's odd to be here, I mean, in the car and driving around and all that."

"Fine," Dorothy said, "That's good. So now maybe we'll get lucky. Stranger things have happened."

There was new silence in the car as if a resting point had been reached, a bargain struck. She wasn't going to say much more. This arrangement was O.K. with me, I suddenly decided. I wasn't all that unhappy driving around in the countryside with her. I spun the knob on the window crank and watched the pines and the splintering lights—I never got tired of the lights. Dorothy tugged at her purse, which was on the seat between us. I stopped her by laying my hand over hers. "What?" I said.

"Cigarette," she said.

"Great," I said. I pulled the purse into my lap and unzipped it. "That's tops. Maybe when you lose your tongue the cigarette won't taste so good, huh?"

"Please."

"Coming," I said. I lit a cigarette and handed it over and when she was smoking and I was working the knob again, I said, "You married now?"

She said, "I'm taking a sabbatical. I have a few friends, a couple of friends. It's all very low-key."

"That's pretty orthodox," I said.

"I've got a fifteen-year-old daughter by my first husband. Her name's Kelly but they call her Jumbo—his mother's idea. Every person in his family was given the ugliest name anybody could think of. It must've been a game they played with each other." Remembering this amused her. There was a tiny smile tracing the corners of her mouth and something shining in her eye. "Or maybe they just didn't know any better. So they got Irma, Bubba Lee, and Sister— that was the first time I'd ever heard of anybody being named Sister, really named that, I mean."

"I guess it is kind of depersonalizing, isn't it?" I said.

"Well, it happens a lot in Arkansas," she said. "I was with Bubba Lee for a year and a half before I found out about his first marriage. It wasn't a marriage so much as an arrangement between his father and his father's brother, a technique for taking care of some hopeless girl, I guess. But it didn't pan out, and when I met him he was free as a bird.

So I married him and eight months later had Jumbo," Dorothy said. "I had to leave her just to get out. I was going to try and go back someday, but I never did."

"How long? Since you saw her?"

"Fourteen years," Dorothy said. "He told me he didn't think it was important that I see her. And I'd given up custody. He didn't know how to have a kid. I guess he thought it was a game. I asked why he hadn't let me get an abortion and he said it was against God's will and he didn't think his mama would like it much, either. I was fifteen. My mother told me I was lucky to get a man who could take care of himself and me both, and that I should shut up and do better housework. 'A man likes a good, clean house,' my mother always used to say. 'A man likes to come home to a nice place so he'll have something to dirty up.' She was the type of woman who thought she knew something about the philosophy of sexual relations."

"A great mother," I said.

"Sure, if you like self-hatred, doubt, fear, loneliness, groveling, and suicide. She'd done that last one before Bubba Lee and I had our first anniversary."

.   .   .

Dorothy drove us down a thin red-clay road through the woods to an abandoned rail tanker depot that had been invisible from the highway. I was ready to get back, but then shrugged and let it go. She drove us straight through a pinch of tight pines to a big clearing at one end of which were a couple of grizzled wood buildings the size of houses, complete with vintage train insignia. The rest of the clearing was fractured concrete slabs a hundred feet wide and huge, squat, once-silver cylinders, maybe ten of them, each one as big as a gymnasium. We got out of the car and sat on the fenders staring out into the darkness at that cracked concrete, and the looming cylinders with the remains of stairs on their sides, and the rusty, stone-and-weed-strewn track. Dorothy lighted a new cigarette off the one she was finishing, then popped the old butt in a pretty arc out in front of us and we watched the sparks fly.

"I suppose I'd better get to it," she said. "People foul things, you know? That's why I brought you out here. I have stuff I want to say, I guess. I want to say something about all the jerks claiming their territory, guys with their dicks over their shoulders, and their brains in their dicks. Guys who think—who really believe—they're ahead of the game. They make me want to pack it in, leave it to them, let them work each other over."

"Easy," I said.

"Well," Dorothy said, leaning back on her fender, looking up at the starry night. "It gets a tad thick out here, you know. I'm four weddings in and I've got an idea of the range of possibilities and let me tell you, there's an argument for living alone."

"Ray?" I said.

"Not really. The rest were worse, does that tell you something? Ray was a pushover compared to the others. After him was Richard, who was this big-and-tall man who thought he knew something about women, thought pussy was real important. I gave him more pussy than he knew what to do with, almost recycled him, but his brain got into the picture. He started thinking big thoughts. That was interesting. That was like watching a seal balance pellets. He thought women were wicked and manipulative, for example. That was a quality thought of his. He made a big stink about that, all the while looking mournful and wounded. Richard did a better mournful and wounded than just about anybody. Classical actors don't do it as well. See, the women made him that way, get it? He was a guy who thought thinking a woman was a great piece of ass was thinking something elemental, something deeply masculine and real. I know that's hard to imagine, but there it is. He used to say Fucking Is Fundamental, you know, a take on the Reading Is Fundamental stuff. He thought that was clever."

"What'd he do for a living, Richard?"

"Who cares? Richard was an artist, quite successful, I guess. Took his act on tour all over this great land—he was a burlesque of a serious person, only people didn't recognize the burlesque part. I loathed him. He was so phony, such a cheat. I mean, I don't mind if a guy gets by with stuff, but there's a point where it's too much."

"Yes," I said. "I've had that same thought. Maybe we should get married and live happily ever after."

"What a nice idea," she said.

I was worried by that, the way it worked, so I thought I'd keep things moving. "What happened after Richard?"

"After Richard I killed a guy."

She turned to look at me across the hood of the Chevrolet, to see how I would react to that. She was sort of breathtaking in that light, in that peculiar twist of her head and her body on the car fender.

"Well, I wish I had," she said. "He was a guy who liked to hit people, me in particular. I think I talked back too much—I may have, really, I mean. I may have taunted him after a while. Anyway, one night when he came after me I waved a kitchen knife around a lot, screamed at his ass real seriously. He kept coming until I caught him on the arm with the knife, just a small cut but it bled like mad. Scared his ass to shit. He went out and brought charges, can you believe that? They did an inquiry, took depositions, but finally this detective said I ought to forget it and sicked a social worker on me."

When she was telling me this about her fourth husband I was thinking that I wanted to make love with her then and there, on the front fender of the Chevy, or out on that concrete, or in the grass alongside it. Somewhere right out there in the open. I wanted to hold on to her and bury myself in her and never let go. This wasn't the sort of thing I felt routinely. It was something about this particular woman who had walked into my motel room unannounced, who had spent an hour or two telling me about herself, who had driven me out into the middle of nowhere for God knows what reason, as if there was a reason, as if there had to be one. She was just enough to be heartbreaking.

Usually I find the reasons not to be attracted to women pretty quick. I see flaws the way other people find things to hope for, things to dream about at night. I see hairs I'm supposed to overlook on the face I'm supposed to love. I see small bruises and I wonder too much where they came from. I smell smells that are better forgotten, whisked away on a friendly breeze. I see faults in eyeliner, clinging hunks of mascara, errant lipstick, badly chosen colors, stinky hair, splotched skin, hanging fat, bad arms—I see what I'm not supposed to, ordinarily, but in Dorothy I saw only possibility, someone to hold tight, that night, anyway. The next night would have to account for itself. I had an idea which way it would go, but it was by no means a sure thing going in, and if it ended badly it would probably be as much her choice as mine. I liked her a great deal. I rolled off my fender and started the long walk toward hers.

. . .

At dinner later, at a restaurant on the highway, Dorothy said, "You ought to go back, get back with Lily. There's no reason to let it go. It's worse with nobody. Most of the time it's worse."

"Is this the time for that?" I asked. "Is this the new guilt?"

"I'm trying to help," she said, matter-of-factly.

"I like to touch you," I said. It was an awkward thing that just came out of nowhere. First I was embarrassed, then proud I'd said it. It was true.

"Ditto," she said.

"And I don't like to touch people as much as I used to," I said, instantly aware that I was losing her, that my interestingly awkward talk had already slipped back to conventional. "Wait a minute, that's not what I mean. Something like that but that's not it."

"It's O.K.," she said. "I like a man who loves his business. I don't believe I'll sleep with you again, though."

I gave her a colorless smile, something protecting me, not her. "As good as that?"

She did a fatigued shrug.

"Sorry," I said. "What about future visits? I may make the ape factory the center of my run up the corporate ladder."

"Thank you, sir," Dorothy said. "You really are nice, aren't you?"

"It's easy when you mean it. I like you."

"Does that answer my question? People like people all the time. It's in many of the modern young novels by our modern young writers. They see it, apparently, a great deal. More than us. Either that or they mean something else."

"I think I must be getting confused," I said. "Were we just out in the country a while ago? At a locomotive site, fallen into disuse? You and me on the car, the ground, so forth? Was that us?"

"It was," she said, grinning. "Exactly us."

"Good," I said. "I feel better. So what is the rest of this stuff you're talking?"

"Optimism? Love of the self? Awareness of the other? Self-defense?" She was especially pretty there and then, in the gentle light.

"Well," I said. "For my part, over here we've got the hopes we've always had. They never change."

She said, "Oh, yeah? Now look who's gone water-walking. What hopes? You're a little guarded, aren't you?"

"It's fine," I said. "Take it private, keep it private. Is that dull? I guess that's dull. I apologize."

We left the restaurant and went out to the car, moving slower than usual because we both knew what was coming. Dorothy drove me to my motel, put me right back where she'd found me. There was a moment in the parking lot when I thought she wanted me to stick with her, maybe follow her to her house, but I knew better when she was rolling again, heading for the parking exit. She stopped at the street and gave me a long last look and I made a gesture that must've looked like semaphore but was supposed to mean why didn't she come back, why didn't we stay together longer, the night, anyway, but she only waved and disappeared into the traffic, leaving me with my wet-look motel parking lot and my tall white lights.

I made my way around the building and up to the second-floor room on the outside of the wing looking away from the pool. I set the air-conditioning thermostat at unbearably cold, dropped my clothes, popped out the power-knob of the television, climbed into the jumpy double bed with the brown comforter pulled up high and my back propped against a swarm of pillows, and I sat there staring at the moving picture, knowing that the next day I was going to feel bad, and I was going to talk to Lily.

13 Out in front of the under-construction airport I got a beat-up Yellow Cab, a Ford I guess it was, something disreputable-looking driven by a kid who himself looked sixteen and real smart. He had the complexion. I gave him my address and settled into the sticky plastic of the rear seat, thinking I'd use the drive to collect myself, but it turned out the kid-driver wasn't going to leave me alone.

"You got family here in town?" he wanted to know. He was looking at me in the rearview, his chin up. I met his eyes once, then just stared at his three-quarter profile over the seat back. He had a few pimples, nothing clinical, and the clean look you can only get from living that way. I was impressed.

"I guess," I said.

"You want me to hurry up?"

"No hurry," I said. "You take it nice and easy, O.K.?" A few billboards slipped by, looking tired and untended and ineffective. A mangled-looking Latin guy in a muscle shirt stood on the road alongside a white Dodge pickup from about 1965. The hood was up on this truck. This Mexican guy wanted help and when he saw he wasn't going to get it from us he shot my cabbie the finger; I don't think my guy caught it, but I was watching and gave the Mexican the bird right back, behind my head, as we swept past.

"Friend of yours?" I said from the back. I knew it was trouble but I couldn't resist.

"What's that? Hey? You want to go faster?" he said, jacking up his chin to catch my eye in the rearview. "You got the time? You got a watch?"

I said, "It's eleven past eleven. Maybe eleven-twelve."

"Whatever you want," he said, pushing the throttle down. The Yellow did a leap, not a great big knock-your-eyes-out leap, but something. Punched me back a little.

"Hey," I said.

"So what are you saying?" he said.

"Nothing. Never mind. Everything's O.K."

"Great," he said, giving it everything he had.

. . .

I got back hating the house on sight, feeling like shit, thinking I'd made a mess of things. I liked Dorothy but that was it. She was interesting, odd, but not a big player in my future. I spent some time figuring out what to do about Lily and finally decided that telling her what had happened was the only thing that made sense, so I called her at midnight and went over there. I told her about Dorothy. I felt like a kid going to confession. I said I was sorry.

We knew these roles.

Lily was nice. First she wanted to know about condoms. Then she said my timing was not good. Then, after sitting there together for a while, silent, she said she guessed guilt was worse. "You did what you wanted and you probably don't do that often enough," she said. "It's O.K. A person should do that kind of thing, stay in touch with himself that way. You need to be able to want what you want and then get it." She looked at me as if waiting for a response, for agreement. I didn't move. Then she said, "Thus the Church of the Healthy Jesus rationalizes poison in the pure body of the marriage."

"Umm," I said.

"Fuck you," she said.

14 There were people all over Lily's house, friends of hers, people I'd never met, or met and forgotten. She was hosting a party, a reception for her supervisor, a guy named Ralph who was moving up to the state level, out of the arts business entirely, and probably wanted to take Lily with him, though according to her he hadn't said a word about it yet. Lily had called in the afternoon to invite me. We had spoken several times since my Birmingham report, but we hadn't seen each other. From the tone of our talks, however, it seemed as if the trip and the intrigue with Dorothy was having this odd effect, the reverse of what you'd expect, pulling us back together, reminding us of each other, making us closer than we had been in months.

On the phone I said, "I want to come, O.K.? But these people of yours, well, you know how they *believe* everything? They drive me crazy. They're so confident. They miss half of what's said because they think they know everything that could be said. I don't know if I should come, Lily."

"I forgot about this," she said. "Maybe you'd better go to a movie instead."

"I can't. I don't have my metallic-blue Volvo, my two children, both beautiful, my lifetime subscription to *Mother Jones.*"

"Well, that's a powerful argument." There was a blank space on the phone and then she said, "I just wanted to call, Peter. I'd like to see you. Come if you feel better. Ray's coming."

I spent the afternoon worrying whether or not to go. We'd settled quickly into the way things were now, to the point of shedding a bit of intimacy—when we saw each other now it sometimes felt like once-best friends getting together after the fact. By dinnertime I had decided to go to the party, so I cleaned up and got dressed in a new suit I'd bought for no reason at all, an expensive suit, double-breasted and Italian. It was a year or two off the pace, but I liked it anyway, I felt like I was holding the line on tradition and quality. Even with the suit, when I got to the house I still wasn't in my best mood.

I lost Lily first thing. She met me at the door, gave me a good hug, and then was off showing Ralph, who had arrived just before me, around the house.

I did a tour, too, back to the bedroom, to the bath, then through the den and dining area into the kitchen. It looked just about the way I remembered it. I was thinking I didn't like Ralph, who was big, physically big, and dapper, too; and I didn't like his friends, not one of them. They were all so correct and with-it and charming and sincere. I wanted to sit down with Lily. To rest. These people were always too clean, too well-groomed, too earnest and caring and genuine. I figured after a certain amount of announced earnestness nausea set in; not so Lily's co-workers. They never ceased to be earnest and caring.

I was trying to get with the program, but I wasn't doing a great job of it. I kept reminding myself how I'd been getting over the bitterness, how I'd had a genuine revelation in the last couple of months about how I was supposed to live and let live. None of that worked much, so after a half hour of poking what I thought was relatively good-natured fun at the slower guests, things got awkward enough so that it was easier to excuse myself than to carry on. I left my bunch poised around a glass-topped coffee table admiring each other's shoes. Sneaker city.

. . .

Somewhere close to ten o'clock I thought I might go out and use the garage apartment, maybe sit in front of the TV out there, take my shoes off, something like that. Maybe I'd sit out there and watch the news and wait for the party to end, and then maybe Lily and I could have a talk—go in the kitchen and clean up after the guests, talk about what had been happening, what we'd been thinking, talk about *things*. So I was on my way to the garage, on the patio, when I noticed a couple by Bud Patrick's fence, the one he'd cut his leg trying to get over. This couple was arm-in-arm and more, in a mobile embrace, leaning against each other, pressing together, veering this way and that as their affection swelled and settled. They were walking and kissing at the same time, which meant shuttling sideways, then moving backwards, then swapping ends and going sideways again, crab-walking, circling without separating, without stopping. I wanted to get out of the yellow light dropped by the patio bulb, so I stepped off the concrete and into the flower bed and the shadows next to the kitchen door. I almost knocked Lily off her feet. "What are you doing?" I said.

"Watching," she said. "How are you?"

I was bobbing, trying to make her out in the dark. She was a couple yards away. "I guess I'm O.K. Aren't you supposed to be inside here? Entertaining the bozos?"

"I'm shirking," she said. "Taking notes on these two out here. This would be my very upstanding employer and his executive assistant. Yvonne Carpenter, I believe. I'll bet Bud's got his infrareds strapped on tonight, huh? You spend lots of time in flower beds?"

I said, "You may not remember me, but my name is Peter Wexler, and I used to live here. This is my house. This is my flower bed, partially."

"Oops," she said, stepping out of the dirt and into the light. "I am sorry. I forgot you were a proponent of owner-oriented marriage. Let me introduce myself, I am your wife, Lily, presently estranged I believe, but everybody calls me Spider."

"What?"

"Many legs," she said, doing a spiderlike curtsy.

I could see her, finally, and she looked lovely. Strangely relaxed, freed. I was stung with feelings for her, shooting around in me like strobe flash; I was intoxicated.

"They don't really call me that," she said. "Nobody ever called me that. I always wanted them to, but they never did. That or Frankie."

"I'll call you Spider," I said. "As a signal of my respect for you and yours."

"I don't want to be called Spider anymore," she said. "I'm over that."

"Whew," I said. "Time passes, doesn't it?"

.   .   .

We went to the garage together. Going up the stairs she kept saying, "I don't know about this." And I kept saying, "It's fine, it's fine." There was a porch running the length of the garage, facing the yard, and we sat up there in director's chairs and watched the couple in the yard below. I brought beer from the tiny red refrigerator she'd repainted.

Lily looked like she was getting younger right before my eyes. She was lanky, well kept. She looked new to me— twenty years of bad skin and she slouched into the chair like a kid of fourteen. "I had to have lunch with them once," she said, pointing toward the yard with her chin. "For cover. It was awful."

As if they'd heard us talking, whispering, Ralph and his friend stopped and stared in our direction. I waved, knowing they couldn't see, knowing they hadn't heard a thing.

I said. "I guess we are estranged, huh? Me and you? Halfway, anyway."

"We're a bit weaned at the moment," she said. "And it's perfectly fine. But I don't want to talk about it today, O.K.?"

"Right," I said.

"Now—Ralph," she said. "I wouldn't mind being estranged from Ralph. He's a head fracture, the way he talks. He's got congenital brainfade, or something. He's a guy who's always behind the nine ball, he's the king of sadness."

"I saw him when I came in," I said. "He looked overcooked."

"Tonight he's got his Mister Curl hairstyle," she said. "The artistic glasses, the well-chosen shirt, the trendy shoes. The watch of the century." She leaned forward to look at the couple on the lawn below. They'd sat down.

"I hate watches," I said. "And I don't like belts much, either."

"Wow!" she said, rocking back. "You sure are interesting. And I like this suit, too. Where'd you get that?"

From down below Ralph said, "Who's up there? Is that you, Lily?"

"Oh my dear God," Lily said. "It's Ralph time."

I said, leaning toward the screen, "Peter Wexler. I live here. Well, I don't really *live* here right now, but I used to. I own it—well, sort of own it. Lily's husband."

"Why not detail our sex life?" Lily whispered.

"Make up your mind, hey?" the voice said. Then there was giggling. Then, "I guess we haven't really met, have we? My name's Ralph Bivens."

Lily whispered, "Bevo to his friends."

"Hi, Ralph," I said, hushing Lily who was right alongside me making faces. "Glad to meet you. Don't let me interrupt you down there. Carry on."

"We were just seeing what was what," he said. "This is Yvonne Carpenter." Then he laughed and said, "Well, I guess you can't see her, but that's who it is. Say hello, Yvonne."

The woman spoke up. "Hi," she said. She had a tiny voice, doll-like, like the voice that comes out after you pull the string on a doll's back.

"Hi, Yvonne," I said. "Nice to meet you."

"Nice to meet you, too," she said.

Right then the patio door opened and Ray stuck his head out and said, "Who the hell's out here doing all the yapping?"

"It's Ray and Judy," Lily whispered.

"Hey, Ray," I said.

"That you, Peter?"

"Yeah, that's Peter all right," Ralph said from down below. "He's upstairs here in the garage. Dreaming that dream."

"Anybody seen Lily?" Ray said. "If you guys see her tell her Uncle Ray's back."

"Why don't you come up?" I called out.

"I'd like to see Lily," Ralph said in a big stage whisper. Then he and Yvonne giggled.

.   .   .

Ray came up. I tried to discourage the other two, but they wanted to come, so they followed Ray. They were surprised that Lily was there. We did handshakes and embarrassed laughter to get over the fact that Lily had been up there all along.

"I was just kidding, just fooling around about that other thing," Ralph said. "About seeing you and all that, you know?"

"Forget it," Lily said.

"She's trying to keep a low profile," I said, by way of explanation.

Ralph and Yvonne wanted to talk about love. They were new at it, new with each other, anyway, and it was still exciting. Ralph was the guy who tells you things you don't want to know about things you don't want to know about, intimate things about himself and his life, on the idea that public disclosure is required of every earnest man. He told us he was a libertine—"Not an organized libertine," he said. "But that's what I am. That's what I stand for. You saw me and Yvonne going around the backyard here, so you know what I mean. That's where we both are in our heads. Right, Yvonne?"

"You can say that again," Yvonne said.

Ray opened his mouth as if to repeat what Ralph had said, then laughed, starting to lip-synch the words.

Ralph grinned at Ray and said, "It *is* a great life, though, isn't it? It's much better than anything I imagined, or anything I did before." He was making hand gestures, slicing at the air as if cutting away underbrush from around him. "With my first marriage and my second marriage—I didn't have a clue," he said. "You get married, have a baby, have a car, have a job, and everything just gets away from you, lickety-split." Then he put an arm around Yvonne's shoulder, tugged her toward him. "Now everything's a lot better. You want something, you take it. That's how we go—bip, bip, bip."

Yvonne rolled her head back against his shoulder, looking up at him affectionately. "Bam, bam, bam," she said.

Both of them laughed.

Lily said, "Well, what is a libertine, exactly?"

She paused to gather up the rest of her question, but Ray beat her to it. "Now, that's not a religious association or anything, is it?" he said. "Is that a tax-exempt thing?"

Ralph leaned forward, separating himself from Yvonne. He had his hands together, his elbows on his knees. He had a genuinely serious look on his face. "You know," he said to Ray. "I sometimes think I *ought* to be tax-exempt. I sometimes think that. I could get something going. But if you do that then you got people saying you're wrong, blaming you, and you know, in a certain way, being a libertine is a relief from all that. I mean, I just don't think about it much anymore. I've got Yvonne, here"—he fingered her shoulder—"and we do what we want, when we want, and where, and that's the whole ball of wax."

"Bam," Ray said.

"Et cetera," I said.

"That's nice," Lily said. "That's really nice. I wish that was the way it was for me. But most of the time, nowadays, at night, I just sit there until something else happens, a new show or something, a telephone call."

Yvonne gave her a funny look. "Or a bath or something like that, right? Is that what you mean?"

"Yeah, a bath," Lily said.

"I get that way a lot," Yvonne said. "Sometimes I'll be somewhere, like at somebody's house or something, and I'll just get a craving for a bath, and I'll just go into the bathroom and take one. Just like that. Sometimes it's a shower, sometimes a bath. Either one."

.   .   .

Ralph and Yvonne climbed down the stairs just about the time Judy made it out onto the patio looking for Ray. He whistled to get her attention and then told her to come upstairs. When we'd resettled in the chairs Ray reintroduced Judy. She said, waving toward the back door into which Ralph and Yvonne had vanished, locked in contact with each other, "This is the guy you work for? This Ralph guy?"

"He's not as bad as he seems," Lily said. "I don't want to defend him, but he used to be a friend."

Ray said, "Somebody pointed him out to me earlier, when I was looking for you guys. The party's for him, right?"

"He seems like kind of a goober," Judy said.

"Judy must not like him much," Ray said. He tapped Judy's forehead as if to check to see if her brain was working. "Maybe you think my sister is just out here to cool down, to shake out her shorts?"

"Jesus," Judy said, zigzagging her face at Ray, then taking a poke at him. "I apologize for my friend. He's always saying stuff he thinks makes him sound interesting. He's a real individual."

"He's probably a libertine," I said.

"What?" she said.

"Nothing. Ralph was just telling us what a libertine he is, how he just mows 'em down, does the right thing. He's hot, he says."

"Me, too," Ray said. "That's me all over."

"It's hard to be hot in the suburbs," Lily said, smiling at me. "Sometimes I'd like to be all steamed up and crazy, but that's almost impossible—you've got your dishwasher, your Maytag, your microwave . . . everything's working against you."

"I rent," Ray said. "When I want to be hot and crazy."

"Yeah," Judy said. "Heaters. He rents heaters. Hundreds of them."

.   .   .

Ray had a new Ford Taurus, so we took that to the yogurt shop to get waffle cones. Lily acted as if she was worried about leaving the party but we convinced her, Judy convinced her.

Gayla was at the yogurt place wearing lemon-colored bicycle pants and a black halter top; she looked like a college girl. Ray couldn't take his eyes off her. Judy slugged Ray a couple of times, three times, and they laughed together about it. I pretended to read a double-fold brochure about the nutritional value of the new, low-fat yogurt; I wasn't going to say anything, but then Gayla caught my eye and I could see she recognized me, so I introduced everybody. When I'd finished Ray asked her what her name was again.

"Gayla," the girl said. "Who are all you guys? Are you at the university?"

"I am," Ray said. "Sometimes."

"Oh," she said, switching to me. "How about the Wal-Mart man? How you doing? Teeth O.K.? How's that boy of yours?"

I tried to explain to the others about taking Charles to get the radio-control truck and running into Gayla and the peanut brittle, but nobody listened, they just did catcalls and flopping eyebrows and let it go.

Gayla was on foot, no bike, so Judy offered her a ride. The five of us got into the Taurus. Ray was telling Gayla how he and Judy were libertines. "We're not exactly there yet," he said. "But we're working on it." The three of them were in the front seat; Lily and I were in the back.

Lily tapped my knee and whispered, "My, we have been busy, busy, busy, have we not?" Then she said to Ray, "Some of us in the back have decided that we think we ought to go bowling."

"Great!" Judy said.

I said, "Wait a minute. Why are you saying that, Lily?"

"I just thought about it," she said. "Why? You think I should go back to the party? You think I can't bowl like any other living being?"

Gayla said, "Party? You guys left a party?" She had a banana split in a quart cup and she was eating as if she hadn't eaten for weeks. It was getting on her face in pretty ways.

"Yeah, but it wasn't a good party," Lily said.

"That's why we left," Ray said.

"I didn't think it was that bad," Judy said. She leaned over and whispered something in Gayla's ear, and the two of them started laughing, looking over their shoulders at Lily and me.

Ray laughed, too, though it was somehow clear that

he didn't know what Judy had said, that he was just pretending to know.

"I guess it would have to be wall-to-wall chainsaw guys to keep me away," Gayla said.

"She doesn't look it, but she's about twenty."

We went over a couple of freeway overpasses, one right after the other, each with glistening razor-wire twirled on top of the fence that was supposed to prevent the kids from diving off, or from painting "Louie Loves Louie" and "Scar Tissue" all over the newly resurfaced concrete.

Something was wrong with Gayla's head—it was oddly shaped, like a spade, a shovel. It was flat on top. I was pointing this out to Lily when Ray caught me in the rearview and gave me eye motions that meant "Cut it out."

"Do you really want to go bowling?" he said, still looking at me in the mirror.

"I don't," I said. I turned to Lily, "We don't, do we?"

"We'll have to get socks," Gayla said. "I'm not wearing anybody's leftover socks."

"Me neither," I said.

Ray said, to her, "What are you, modern? Why don't you go live in New York, where it pays to be modern."

"Doesn't pay as much as it used to," Gayla said. "I just moved back from there, anyway. I was in school."

"What school?" Lily said.

"I forget," Gayla said. "Art school, I think. Love school. I was on a love crusade."

"She forgets," I whispered to Lily, who slapped me for my trouble, just a pop on the shoulder, but I liked it. For a second I imagined sex with Gayla, but I felt bad about it. It was one of those things that happens so fast you don't have any time to stop it. I don't always think stuff that way, but it happens. You think something and then feel bad—

it's beneath you, or disgusting; but there's nothing really wrong with thinking stuff you don't try to think but zips through your brain anyway. That stuff's like dreams—you're not responsible.

"Aren't you young for a love crusade?" Ray said.

"Depends what you mean," Gayla said.

Lily gave me another small punch. "I'm sort of the Mike Tyson of love, myself," she said. "Banging away at 'em until they drop." Then she hit Ray on the back. "And I don't want to go bowling, Ray. Everybody goes bowling when they want to slum, when they want to get back. I hate that—Ernie K-Doe and the Chantels. Forget it. It's out."

"Bowling's out," I said to Ray.

"What?" He turned sideways in the seat and drove that way, facing Gayla and Judy, watching the road over his left shoulder. "No bowling? What are we going to do? Maybe we should go to the love store?"

Gayla said, "What's with you, chum?" It sounded mean and fundamental, and it stopped all of us for a minute.

We went to the Big Boy and ordered chicken-fried steak, which they insisted, wrongly, on calling country-fried. Ray wanted to order "Tiny English" peas, which he insisted he'd had there before, but, as it turned out, they had no peas, "Tiny English" or otherwise. That's when Judy told us Ray had a temper. "He throws things and screams," she said.

"Who doesn't?" Gayla said, snapping her fingers almost in Ray's face. "It seems like everybody's always mad about something."

Ray fidgeted with his water glass, then looked at Judy, who was across the table. "I'm meditating," he said. "I saw this movie about the sixties on television, so now I'm trying it out again. Everybody meditated back then."

Judy lifted her glass and wagged it at him. "Hand me some new ice, will you?"

He gave her a look, then took the glass across to the silver ice machine by the window.

"Short legs," she said, watching Ray walk. "Another couple of inches in the thigh and bang! Mr. Hermano Perfecto."

"Why, thank you, Judy," Ray said. "That's very giving and charitable of you." He dipped her glass in the open ice chest. "Now, about young Gayla there, she is cute, isn't she? Young and cute?"

"Endangered," Lily said.

"Not at all," Judy said. "Ray? Come back over here and settle down. Come on."

Ray did a sweeping dance step, a waltz step, on the way back. "I'm harmless," he said to Gayla. "I'm a romantic."

"I thought you were a libertine," she said.

"Same thing," he said.

"That was two other fellas," I said.

Judy was drawing water-animals on the plastic tabletop. "Last night we go to dinner at this place and this girl he used to know, a girl named Helene, a pupil or something, slips up behind him and starts smooching all over his neck. Right in front of me."

"Where's Ralph when we need him," I said to Lily.

"Hush," she said.

Ray slipped Judy's glass in front of her and said, "Go on, Judy."

"We'd just started dinner and Helene slides up, shakes her booty, and then goes for his neck. I wanted to flatten her," she said. "But I sit there and smile, and after a time I wag my hand around in front of my face like I'm after a fly or something, thinking the girl will get the signal. Thinking *Raymond* will get the signal. Nobody does."

"I was trying to get the signal," Ray said.

"You weren't doing a thing," she said, turning to me as if I alone understood what she was saying. "I'm sensing everybody's eyes on me, you know? In the restaurant. They're waiting for me." Judy took a bite of ice and turned around for a look at our empty Big Boy. "She's got on the leather jacket, you know, like from a few years ago—I mean the girl's seen a *lot* of Pontiac advertising. So she looks up from behind Ray's shoulder, looks right at me, and I can see this smile, these eyes, gleaming, like she's having a great time."

"This is spooky," Gayla said.

"She has these watery green eyes," Judy said. "Ray-gun eyes."

"So tell us what happened and get it over with," Lily said.

"We had dinner with her," Ray said. "That's what happened. We sat there and watched her eat for an hour. That's it. Judy wouldn't eat a thing."

Judy sighed theatrically and put her head down on the table. "We had dinner with her," she said. "Way to go, Ray. Way to queer the deal."

"Well? We did."

"Yes. I know we did. We heard all about her life. We know where she works now. We know there's nothing sinister about her, there's no mystery. We saw pictures of her boyfriend and his two kids, I swear."

"That's true," Ray said. "Ugly fucks."

"She's a med tech," Judy said. "She works at the Pathology Lab. Do you know what she does? She sits in a room the size of a closet and puts stuff on microscope slides.

Human tissue and worse than that, I'm not saying what. I didn't believe her until she showed me her badge. You know, she has to wear a badge around, to show that she belongs."

Ray hit his fist softly on the table. "I always wondered about that. I mean, what sort of job is that? Glass things all lined up, one new disease after another. I mean, what's a girl like that do for excitement?"

Judy shook her head. "Well, I guess she just kicks way back and remembers you, Starman."

.   .   .

We ate fast. It was as if nobody wanted to eat, but we didn't know it until the food was on the table. It wasn't long before we were back in the car, headed for Lily's.

I was thinking that it was probably my fault we'd never made friends with the Regulars of the world, the ones who follow the rules and go home when they're supposed to, stick with spouses and families, go to church, believe everything's going to be all right. I said to Lily, "I wonder how the party turned out?"

She shrugged. She looked tired.

Gayla came climbing over the seat so she could sit in back with us. "You're acting too old," she said to me. Then, trying to get Lily to agree, she said, "Lily is not going to be sexually intrigued if you keep acting old."

"Oh, you never know," Lily said. "He's not too bad for an old guy." She let her head rest against my shoulder.

"Good answer," Ray said, turning around to give Lily his personal approval. "That makes me feel great to hear you say that, you know? It's like *I'm* not really dead, either."

"He thinks he's dead," Judy said, turning around.

"He is," Lily said. "I was talking about Peter. I wasn't talking about him at all. Not in any way."

15 I ran into Bud Patrick outside the Blockbusters video store the week after the party. He wanted to talk, so we got into a conversation that started at the counter and went on until we were out on the sidewalk. He'd noticed I wasn't around the house much anymore.

"So what happened?" Bud asked. "You and Lily calling it quits?"

"I don't know what we're doing, Bud," I said.

"Well, don't do anything rash," he said. "O.K.? People always make these snap decisions and then they regret the hell out of them later, know what I mean?"

"I know what you're saying," I said.

"Take me, for example," he said.

"No thanks, Bud." It was a risky joke, but I tossed caution to the winds. We weren't best friends, anyway. I said, "So to speak. That was just a term of art, Bud. That was a figure of speech."

"I knew that," he said.

Bud had on a big white shirt, Latin American style,

easily two sizes too big for him, and he was a big one. I said, "Where'd you get this shirt? What is this, a new shirt thing you're into here, something I don't know about?"

"If you don't know about it it's your own fault," he said. "I've been reading up and this is the thing of the moment, this shirt right here. The latest. Got it from that *International Male* catalog—shirt came all the way from Sweden."

"They're wearing those in Sweden now, eh? They got a lot of barbers in Sweden?"

Bud shook his fat head and smiled, letting it go. "What's that you're getting there?" he asked, poking his three brown-boxed video tapes at the one I had.

"Porn," I said. "I've given myself over to it entirely. I've decided to become a sex addict, Bud, what do you think about that?"

He didn't think much. "Keep it a secret," he said, waving at me as he started toward his car. "We all have them, you know. In the meantime, I'll keep an eye on the home-stead for you, O.K.?"

"Thanks, Bud," I said.

He stopped alongside his car and straightened the long squared-off tail of his shirt, then looked back at me. "You really think this looks stupid? I mean, am I going around here looking like a bozo?"

"Nah," I said, flicking a hand at him. "It's fine. I was just messing with you. It's O.K., really."

I watched him get into his car and start it up. He backed out of his slot and I stood there on the sidewalk, watching him. He had to pull in front of me to get out of the lot and when he did I bent over, stabbing my forefinger against the video box I had, and I yelled, "Weather. It's a weather tape. Rain." I made rain motions with my hands, dragging them

16

At six-thirty I drove over to the grocery store where Lily and I always shopped together. I parked a fair distance from the door, next to a light standard, a pole eighteen inches in diameter with twelve unequal sides and eight nuts the size of mini-doughnuts on eight bolts as big around as my thumb. I parked there and stared at this pole and thought about a time years before when Lily and I were getting back together after I'd had a particularly messy affair. It was an evening when I had driven Lily to another grocery store, a Safeway store on a street named Dunlavy. We had a Ford sedan, a four-door, that we had just bought from a friend of hers, and we were at the store buying groceries for a Friday night barbecue. She went in to pick up the hamburger meat and the frozen steak fries, and I stayed in the car in the parking lot. It was a summer Friday. There were a lot of people out, a lot of people with ideas like ours—a cookout, a few friends sitting on the deck together drinking beer and enjoying what there was to enjoy. We had a pine deck in those days, can-tilevered off the back end of our duplex apartment.

That day as I sat in the parking lot waiting for her and watching people drift into and out of the Safeway, several things hit me, chief among which was that the people I was watching were very pretty, both the women and the men. Even then it was clear to me that this was new, different than when I was young, and I was curious as to how this whole generation got to be so much better-looking than mine. These people seemed light and healthy, and the way they moved across the blacktop had a certain elegance. There were a lot of cut-off jeans, loose shirttails—Hawaiian shirts were already a hot item. The women were thin and tan, thin and tan. All of them. And happy, even though it was just very early summer, it was May maybe, at best. The tans were so good that I assumed they were faked, stuff out of a tube that if you get it wrong you look like your mother was neon and your father was a fish.

Anyway, as the couples came out the men were usually acting powerful, like muscle guys and know-it-alls, swaggering, leading their women, carrying more big bags of groceries than necessary. Guys carried four, even five bags. Of course, that wasn't everybody. In a few couples you could see liberation leaping forward, you could measure it by the distribution of the bags.

Lily was in the store getting hamburger meat and beer and buns and steak fries and beans. And barbecue sauce, of course. And in each case she was getting our preferred brand, whatever it was at the time. In potatoes it was Ore-Ida, I remembered. But in every case without exception she was buying a specific brand, a brand that meant something to us because we liked the way it tasted, or because we'd made a joke about it when we first saw it, or because we thought the people who made it were less horrible than the people who made a competing product, or because her mother or my mother introduced us to it, or because some other sentimental value was associated with it, or because the commercial for it was particularly charming or funny or wonderful in a way we wanted to align ourselves with, or for any of fifty other reasons that attracted us to a particular brand-name product in a particular product category. We didn't, for example, buy just any old brand of paper towels. No, we had very clear feelings about paper towels, deeply held feelings, so that if we had to have paper towels we would always get the same brand of paper towels, sometimes even leave one store and go to another to get this brand, and the reason about paper towels was that our brand was *better* than the other brands. No other factors entered into the decision.

Ray was scheduled for dinner, along with a woman who lived across the street, a woman named Jane who I'd wanted to sleep with, but it hadn't happened, and now I was glad.

I guess you could have thought that ours was a marriage in trouble even back then, what with the affairs—Lily had had two; I'd had the one we were getting over—but it wasn't, or didn't seem like it. In fact, I was so happy to be out of the situation with Sheila that it was hard to express that happiness without getting unbearably corny. Up until that point Lily and I had been together almost five years, and both of us seemed content with the prospect of the rest of our lives together. With the prospect of buying one bungalow after another on into eternity. With the prospect of trading up on our Ford sedan, and on the sedan after that, and the sedan after that.

So then—still sitting, still watching—I began to think that life was so sweet, in fact, with Lily and myself, things so good, so perfect, now that we were back together and I was done with Sheila, and that Lily had handled it brilliantly making me love her even more—she was hurt without being hysterical—that it suddenly occurred to me that it might be a good idea to go ahead and have an affair with Jane just so Lily and I could reconcile again afterward. I didn't know if anybody ever did anything like that, but it seemed such a great idea that I started the car and slipped it down into Drive, and then rolled on by the grocery and down to the drugstore where there was a telephone on a pole outside, and I pulled the car up to that pole and reached out and got the handset, punched my quarter into the slot, and dialed Jane's number then and there.

It scared me a bit, because in the midst of all that happiness I was thinking crazy stuff, stuff you always say but never do—who ever quits while he's ahead?

Anyway, Jane answered and I chickened out, just reminded her that dinner was scheduled for eight, pretended that was the only reason I'd called. Then I reversed my way back to the spot in front of the grocery to wait for Lily.

.   .   .

So here I was years later remembering all this in a similar parking lot, waiting for Lily to show up just so I could catch a glimpse of her. I thought it was funny that when I'd run into Bud earlier I'd been embarrassed at first to tell him I'd rented a videotape of a thunderstorm—God knows we'd had enough real rain to satisfy anybody but a totally crazed rain junkie. But I'd been thinking a lot about weather, about how much I liked it, about how I wanted to get into the movie business to do weather films, weather documentaries. Weather was so big and embracing that it was worth the trouble. Sitting there in the car next to the lamp standard I let my head roll to the side and leaned it against the door so that out the driver's window I could watch clouds glide across the sky. It was a cloudy day. There wasn't much sky visible for the clouds to go across. It was mostly clouds up there—gray bottoms, whiter tops. Miles and miles of clouds, acres of clouds, thundering across the sky. So big. I don't know what got into me, but I was stolen away by these clouds, by the way they kept moving, never stopped, never slowed, never altered course. I was cloud hungry, cloud mad. I remembered that once, when I was just a kid, my father caught me watching the sky, and he said to me, "Boy! Quit your staring at that sky. You can't make no living out of staring at the sky."

I guess he'd never heard of agriculture.

I started thinking about the way these Latino guys you always see on TV or in the movies wear these long-sleeved shirts over plain white T-shirts, and how they button only the top button of the outer shirt and leave the shirttail out, so that there is an inverted "V" going up their chests, the apex of which points to their chins. I was thinking about that, thinking of trying it myself, wondering if my peers and colleagues at the office, not to mention Lily, might think something new of me if I tried that, wondering what Ray would think, or what Bud Patrick would.

I sat in the car thinking about shirt situations I might try out, looking at the clouds, wondering whether Lily was ever coming, wondering if I'd missed her.

Sheila, the woman I'd had this timid affair with years before, had been nineteen and a graduate student in polymer science, a great new science that they hadn't even had when I was in college. She knew more about polymers than anybody I ever met. You'd walk down the street with Sheila and she'd start touching things, poking things, pointing stuff out, saying, "That's a polymer. That's a polymer. That's one, too." Thing after thing that you thought was steel or aluminum or rubber or another natural material would turn out to be polymer when you were in Sheila's company. I swear to God that you'd see something that for all the world looked like a piece of wood, maybe Piranha Pine or something, as pretty as a picture, and you'd run a finger along it and bang! Sheila was right there telling you it was polymer-based.

It was on one such walk with Sheila that I first understood that the world had changed. I was behind her, watching her calves, watching the way they flexed when she stepped, and she was pointing out the polymers in the usual way, and I just suddenly thought it: "This isn't my world, anymore." It's a curious sensation to describe, this moment in which you realize your sole proprietorship has been breached, your purchase on the world around you has given way, that you no longer obtain, so to speak, that not only are you not a primary force in the culture, but your group is not a primary force, not even in the small way in which it was, formerly. It's that moment when you know beyond any doubt that whatever it is you think about anything, about any cultural or historical or theoretical thing, whatever you think about politics and personal relations and government and clothing, movies, art, theology, sociology, whatever it is, *it just doesn't matter,* period. That's a bad moment and the only comfort is that it happens to everybody, it even happens to people who don't notice that it's happened to them. If you do notice it's heart stopping, it's like somebody points a finger at you and says, "You. You're out. You're in the way. Move along."

That was it, that was mine, there behind Sheila. Suddenly, distinctly, it wasn't my world, anymore, it was her world, and before long it wasn't even going to be hers, it would be somebody else's. This was when she was nineteen and I was thirty-something.

I remembered all this while I was getting ready to give up on Lily for the night, but I was still sitting and staring absently at the clouds when this old guy came along and started to get into the next car along in the line. Before he got in his he stopped a minute and said, "You O.K., Bud-ro?"

"What?" I said, straightening. "Who're you calling Bud-ro?"

"I was just wondering if you were O.K.," he said.

"Sure. I'm fine," I said. "Don't I look good?"

"You look as if you're having an arrest or something," the guy said. "You look like you're infarcting."

"I'm examining these clouds," I said, and I pointed at the clouds so he would know which clouds I was talking about. "To see what they portend, if they portend anything, which I don't think they do, now, after careful study. I was watching them move. See how they're moving?"

He looked up, squinting. "Yep," he said.

It occurred to me that this was perfect and typical parking lot talk, that people always talked to each other this way in parking lots, there was this familiarity born of the commonness of purpose, the purpose being arriving or leaving. The guy talking to me was an old geezer, I mean, he must've been fifty-five, sixty. He was out of the past, from the ranks of the almost gone, just like me. He had thin arms with red pokey hairs on them, bad Bermuda shorts, eerie knees, and lousy shoes. Leather things, no socks.

He said, "I didn't mean to bother you too much. I was worried. You get as old as me and you start worrying about everything. You worry if the neighbor's car's gonna start, you worry somebody's gonna knock on your door."

"Well," I said. "That's mighty nice of you. But there's no need to worry. I'm out here, uh—I'm waiting on my wife, Lily." I pointed toward the big glass windows that fronted the grocery store. "She's in here getting hamburger stuff. We're having a cookout."

"Whooo-eee," he said. "Isn't everybody? Don't I know it. Look," he said, rattling his shopping bag at me. "I've got a couple of porterhouse steaks in here'll make your eyes lean outta their sockets just for a glimpse, make your eyebrows drive all the way up to Oklahoma."

"In little tiny cars," I said, trying to stay with him.

"Sure, pal," he said. He put one hand on the roof of my car and torqued himself around for a good solid look at my clouds. "A man could get lost in these things," he said. "You want to be careful." He looked at me then with an expression on his face that I didn't quite recognize, an expression of the sort you might make if you had just said something profound, as if you knew something that the person to whom you were speaking did not know. That's the way he looked.

It was unnerving—I'm always perturbed when people make faces at me, especially when they're faces I don't quite understand. I didn't understand him. He wasn't being smug, particularly. There wasn't any reason for him to be smug in the first place, and in the second, he was too strange a bird for smugness. No, I figured he thought—he *knew*—he had said something important. After a time I guessed it was that I was, in his words, lost in the clouds, and I began to wonder if that was true. I mean, what kind of silly marriage is it that permits of, and even encourages, people to move out, to live apart? I began to think that marriage itself was a challenge to all of Western thought from the time of Christ to the present moment. A challenge, at least, to some of

Western thought. Then it became clear to me that this wacky old guy was a sign, some intermediary to whom I was supposed to pay attention if I was to progress in my growth and development as a human being. I figured that he meant I was suffering from too much time in the parking lot, and I guess I was getting pretty spooky, hunkered out there on the blacktop staring at the sky. I didn't usually think much of signs from the beyond, or of intermediaries, but now, at least to the extent that I thought this old guy coming up to me meant I'd better do something about Lily, and to the extent, I suppose, that that was already the direction of my thinking, such as it was, then maybe the time had come to quit screwing around. If I was sitting around outside grocery stores just to get a glimpse of my wife maybe I ought to consider repudiating my old complaints and my new house, maybe I ought to think about getting home.

The old guy gave me a thumbs-up once he got his Dodge going, and I gave him one right back. There was a terrific amount of noise, rumbling, out of the car, and considerable smoke as well, but as he pulled out I turned and looked back through the huge plate-glass windows of the store, windows tinted by the application of thin, clear, greenish-yellow sun-repellent plastic to the inside, and I spotted somebody who looked like Lily standing in line at one of the checkout islands. In front of her, across the glass, I could see the reflections of my clouds, passing from pane to pane. And in the image of this woman who looked like Lily but wasn't Lily I saw something peculiar, a reflection of a sharp spike of light that hit her as she stood in the line, and as I looked at her it was behind her and slightly above and cool white light circling her head like a queer halo, and that seemed to say what I knew or needed to know, and that's when I reached down and started the car.

17

I wanted to tell Lily what I was thinking so she'd have a chance to get used to the idea before it was actually advanced, I wanted to give her a preview of this new idea of mine, that maybe I was over *it,* my problem, my indulgence, so I went to my house and waited a half hour, then called her. It was cold in my house but I was sweating, I was clammy. Pale blue-green light from the neighbor's pool squeezed past the ratty drapes and flickered on the wall of my den. I pushed the wet hair off the back of my neck and sat on the edge of the mattress waiting for Lily to answer. It had started to rain. I liked the way the water sounded, the way it seemed to surround me. I wiped my forehead with the corner of the sheet, then wrapped a bit of it around my neck and slipped it back and forth like a shoe rag. It seemed as if her phone went on for a week. I hung up on the answering machine the first time, then I gave up and left a message, just saying who it was and what time it was.

I rested for few minutes, maybe longer, shut my eyes and lay down half-on and half-off the bed. Then in the bare light of the room I could make out the outlines of my shirts hanging in the open closet, my suitcase on the floor just where it had been since I moved, shoes and pullover shirts still in it. The decoration in this house was profoundly furnished-room. My bedroom had a couple of department store lamps, one a floor model and one a clip-on, and a king-size bed, a rattan chair and ottoman, both with meal-colored cushions, and, opposite the bed, a machine-chiseled wood frame on a mirror. My neck was stiff. A thick seam of pain, not sharp, not pronounced, shifted down the left side of my back. It was seven, seven-thirty. I called again. The machine answered and I left another message, joking to try to make it seem as if I weren't desperate, but knowing that I was dead that way. There was no disguising it.

I thought about going to bed, but knew that even if I could sleep it would only last an hour or two, and that afterwards I wouldn't start my real night until five or six in the morning. That meant reading too many magazines and watching too much featureless television about a guy in a motel room somewhere in the middle of nowhere, happy to be stealing a room and a bed somebody else had to take care of, happy for a few nights alone at the end of winter, and for a six-hour drive the next day, and then another room, another bad restaurant, another gawky trio in a lounge run by a wisecracking parched blonde wearing a too-short black skirt and serving bar liquor to travelers pleased to be talked to and eager to feel at home. TV.

In my dark bedroom the quiet spread out around me like a dense summer night in childhood. I watched the furniture throw its shadows on the carpet. I waited to call Lily again.

. . .

The doorbell went off, a grotesque three-toned thing. I jumped, rubbed my eyes as I got off the bed. I went down the hall and answered the front door. It was Lily. She was smiling. "Surprise," she said.

It was more than that, but I only hugged her, got her inside. She was soaked. I steered her down the dark hall and into the bedroom, gave her a fresh mint-green towel I got from a stack of towels in the bathroom, and showed her my closet.

"Help yourself," I said. "It's amazing you're here, I was just thinking about you. I called you. Twice, maybe three times. You weren't home. I was over at the grocery store and I saw a woman who looked just like you and then I came here and called you. I left a message. Well, the first time I hung up, then I left a message a couple times."

"I'm a popular gal," she said. "I got the message, that's why I came over." She was toweling her arms, then her hair. "You were at the store?"

"In the lot," I said.

"In the lot?" she said. She yanked the towel around her shoulders and turned on the lamp beside the bed. "It's powerful dark in here, isn't it?"

"I guess it is," I said.

I was embarrassed about the way the place looked. She saw that and gave me a smile. "Listen," she said, "I don't know what you think this is, but I just wanted to come by and see you. I mean, is it all right?"

"It's great," I said. "Really. I'm glad you came. I want to talk to you, anyway."

"What about? Big stuff?" she said.

She'd stopped drying and she wasn't changing her clothes so she was standing there soaked and I didn't know if she wasn't changing because I was standing there. "Why don't I go make us coffee," I said. "You can dry off and get yourself straightened away, change or whatever."

Right then she dropped the wet dress around her ankles, stepped out of her panties, started again with the towel, more earnestly this time. "What stuff?"

I was headed out the door, toward the hall. "I'll catch you in the kitchen, O.K.?"

"I'm fine, Peter," she said. She sighed and grabbed one of my cotton robes from the closet, wrapped that around her and carefully folded up the sleeves until she had a pirate-size cuff. Then she followed me close, step for step, her feet making sticky sounds on the fake parquet of the hallway, into the kitchen where we sat at a rickety table I'd picked up at a flea market, a wooden table that had been painted funny. Lily said, "One of the reasons I'm here is I miss you so much. Charles told me that when he stayed over here one time you guys were writing a suicide note and you ended up driving around in the car at three in the morning—is that right?"

"Oh, well," I said. "I guess that was sort of mostly a joke, the suicide thing. And sometimes I go out and sit in the car at night—I like it."

"Sure," she said. "I remember. But this other thing, I mean, I knew it was a joke, but I don't even like you thinking about it, I don't like you operating in the area. You know better."

There was a stupid brown bird, a stupid sparrow, on the ledge outside the kitchen window. There wasn't much of an overhang, so this bird was getting wet, constantly fluttering its feathers to ditch the water.

Lily said, "The girl's been coming around, that kid we went to get ice cream with."

"Who, Gayla?" I said.

"Yeah. First time she asked about you, but since then she comes to see Charles. He's weird about it. She's not that much older than he is, really."

"What are you talking about? She's fifteen or something, isn't she?"

"No, I don't think so," Lily said. "Twelve, tops. It's O.K. They watch television and stuff. They stay in his room a lot, I guess they're playing doctor." She stopped and looked to see how I was reacting to her joke. I wasn't, so she tried to change the subject. "I've been thinking—how's your patience? Can you take this?"

"Sure," I said. "I can take anything. That's what I'm built for. You don't think Charles and Gayla—"

"It's early yet," she said.

"Right," I said. "I knew that. It's just that she's kind of quick, you know? Older."

"It's fine," she said. "Trust me."

"O.K."

"What I wanted to say was I've been thinking things like you lately. Suddenly. I don't know where it came from, but, I mean, all these people pussyfooting around all the time, being polite and practical and friendly and open-minded—it's not attractive. It's stupid and confusing. I've decided that I'm just going to go on and tell the truth as much as I can."

"Within reason," I said. I gave her a coffee cup, empty.

"Well, first, I'm ready to kill some of these pro-life apes. I mean I *really* hate what they're doing. Why should they get to tell everybody else what to do? What, are they privileged or something? Are they better?"

"I don't think so," I said.

"And these puke-boys with their conscientious higher

authority crap—Jesus, I could kill these guys. The ones who go on TV and say somebody is pro-death—even Jesus hates these people."

"Whoops!" I said.

"You also got pro-rape, -abuse, -ritual-murder—that's me all over. But, hey, I guess it takes all types, right?" She shrugged and said, "We're headed backward, Johnny to the Dark Ages, come in with a friend. And why not? Those were the good times—last week I saw a guy on TV going on and on about this woman who was raped and cut up, and he says she was asking for it because she didn't have any panties on. And you know, maybe he was right. Maybe if she'd had her panties on like a good little girl then that poor man who was driven to distraction by the missing panties would have been able to restrain his manliness, to keep it curled up in its little pouch."

"Parked there," I said. "Courtesy of one of this half-century's finest revolutionary minds."

"What? Oh. What's-his-name, right? Anyway, I'm beginning to feel like you."

I said, "You don't have to feel like me. It's O.K."

"Stuff didn't get on my nerves so much," she said. "I never had much say in anything anyway, so I just handled myself and let the rest go. But lately it's grating. I watch a lot of TV news and that's amazing stuff night after night, incredible lies and craziness. I mean, sometimes it seems like it's just one really ignorant thing after another, kind of an unending parade of the despicable, the contemptible, the repulsive. Maybe it's just that since you're not around I'm paying attention; maybe if you were there that'd be enough, I'd have to work against your depressions."

"Thanks," I said.

"Anyway, on abortion, I figure anybody who isn't having one ought to keep her trap shut about anybody who is, and vice versa."

"Check," I said.

"Wait a minute," she said. "I'm not finished." She got up to take a closer look at the bird on the ledge. The bird was fearless, it just stared back at her. She suddenly blushed, looking self-conscious about this talk she'd started, like it sounded too serious to her. "Well, air travel is out," she said. "Period. If they can't do better than they're doing let's tell 'em to forget it. It's a clown show. And we might as well talk to the pilots about moustaches. We've got a problem there. We need a high-school equivalency diploma in the moustache." She looked at me to see how this was playing. I smiled and wiggled my finger in circles, and she obliged: "Unless that's too broad for the academics, who may feel there's not enough secondary material on the moustache. We could include other facial hair, though I personally think that would dilute the integrity."

"Jesus, I know," I said.

"It's serious," she said. "Some of these things look like outtakes from a live-brown-animal-eating contest."

"Village People Syndrome," I said. "There was a piece in *JAMA*. I figure it's a personal statement, kind of 'I am pubic hair, hear me roar.' "

"We've got to go at the news guys on hair, O.K.?" She smiled at me. "I'm sticking with hair, you may have noticed. I think I've got a hair thing. The rules are, first, hair is not a device; second, hair is not an aerobic exercise; third, hair should not look as if it arrived at your door UPS Blue Label from a foreign land where hair is plentiful."

.   .   .

In a comfortable way we started touching each other, playing there in the kitchen, teasing, gently stroking forearms, hands, then kissing a little, hugging, and in a few minutes we were on the floor beginning to make love in a way we hadn't in a long time—eagerly, aggressively, mean but loving; it was the kind of sex that felt like you couldn't get close enough no matter how hard you tried, couldn't get your bodies jammed tight enough together, your mouths open wide enough, couldn't cover enough sweat-slick skin with your hands. It wasn't usual for us now, though there was a time. I don't know why it started, and I don't think Lily expected it any more than I did, but once begun both of us gave ourselves to it with a minimum of self-consciousness, and even that was shared and laughed at, made part of the play. We worked our way through most of the ugly rooms in my rented house and came to rest in the garage nearly an hour later, wrapped in one of the satin packing quilts I'd ordered from somewhere the first year we were married. We'd had one of them, the lilac one, on a wicker couch for a while, but now it was in a box in my garage, and we were grateful. We were stuck together in the quilt, her knee up between mine. I was on my back.

"Here's my South American position," Lily said.

"It's good," I said. "It's hot."

"Not that," she said. "See, I figure there are people down there and those places are their countries. It's a strange concept, I know. But, like, when was the last time you went to Sears, bought forty gallons of blue paint, brought it home and fixed up your neighbor's house for him? Because he really *needed* a blue house, know what I mean?"

"That's correct," I said. "So what about men? Men in general, present company excluded?"

"Men are duck-rabbits."

"Now we're cooking," I said.

"Wait, let's don't be too clever," she said. "You know how they hate it when you're clever. They get nervous. They get worried. They figure you're out to get them somehow."

"We are out to get them, aren't we? Don't we want to punish somebody? Make them crawl and beg and squeal?"

"I knew a guy once who said he liked to fuck women because he loved to hear them squeal," Lily said.

"He should've fucked mice," I said.

"Mice?"

The rain was mostly over, drips and drizzle and that peculiar quiet that seems to follow small storms. We were on the floor of the garage, on flattened cardboard boxes, covered with this quilt. The cars—hers and mine—were in the driveway, and there were lots of overgrown bushes around, so we weren't all that available to passersby.

"O.K.," she said. "Are you ready for the dullest creations of man?" This was a game we used to play. "Huh? Ready? You go first."

"O.K. Uh, the human breast is one," I said. "And, guys who spit, especially the ones who do it in cups."

"I don't want to play anymore," she said.

.   .   .

Then we had our talk. I told her that I loved her as much as ever, that I thought about her all the time, that I walked and talked her, that I heard her laugh when I overheard other women laughing, that I imagined her coming when I heard footsteps, that when I was alone in my house sometimes, sitting in the bed reading or staring at the television, I could feel her there with me, feel her disturbance of the air, I could recall her scent and bring back the balance of the bed with both of us in it. I said I could remember everything, that I was never without her.

"He's a weird one," Lily said. "That guy."

I said, "I thought something would focus itself, but after I got out all it was was missing you, and Charles, all the time. Now I just want to shut up and pay the rent, buy the clothes, get a new car every couple of years, read a newspaper, vote, mow the lawn. I'll be satisfied to clean out a few closets, maybe straighten up the tool shed, take a vacation like a normal person, maybe go to the Grand Canyon, or Lookout Mountain, or Rock City. I want to go to the store with you again and buy the groceries, maybe a roast, maybe a little rib roast. I want to get a couple of new shirts that I like, and maybe get some Chinese food once in a while, maybe pick it up and bring it home and eat in front of the TV."

"So how long is this going to last?" she said. "A couple weeks? Months?"

"I want to get together," I said.

"So do I," she said.

I told her I felt a lot better, I'd learned something, that she'd been on target to start with, that I didn't know why I hadn't gotten it right back then. It was a quiet conversation, looking out toward the driveway of my house, in the night. It was pretty out there. She didn't say much, just that it was O.K., that she wouldn't mind me coming back, that Charles would be happy about it, too. She looked at me when she said that, just to be sure I got it.

I did, and then we held each other for a time, gently, very peacefully, and then we packed it in. She left, went to get Charles and went back to the house. I thought everything was O.K. I thought I'd probably keep my house for a couple of months just to be safe, or because of the lease, or for an unspecified but no less real reason, but that I was going home sooner rather than later. I felt good about that.

18 Ray called and asked how I would like it if he stayed a few days at my place. It had been a while since the Birmingham specialty and the talk with Lily. Most of my stuff was boxed. It was late in the afternoon and raining again. I was walking around in red cotton socks and thinking about starting a fire because we'd had so much chilly rain, fall rain, with fine, whitish drops. There was flooding, trees were down, the power had gone off a few times. The city was a mess, they said on television.

Lily had phoned minutes earlier to tell me the oil light in her car was blinking and she had stopped at a Star station to get it checked. She'd be late, she said.

She was coming over to cook dinner, which she'd done a couple times recently. This time Gayla and Charles were taking in a film, a foreign film, I'd been told, at the mall CinePlex. Gayla's mother was picking them up at the theater. Then Charles was spending the night at Gayla's house because of something they were planning the next day, though I never got exactly what it was. A science fair project, maybe. I'd also learned that Charles was thinking of changing his name to Laramie. He thought that sounded good, sounded rough and tumble. I'd asked Lily to set up a meeting between the three of us to go over a few things.

"So what do you say?" Ray said on the phone. "I've got to get out of my apartment for a bit. We're doing what you guys did, taking time off." He sounded uncertain, I guess because I'd waited too long to say yes. He said, "I talked to Dorothy."

"Good news travels," I said.

"It's O.K.," he said. "I'm not worried about it. I just need a break over here—we need one."

"Well, sure, you can stay. It's fine. Is Judy O.K.?" I was listening to the traffic in the background, trying to figure where he was calling from.

He said Judy was perfect, and nothing in the world was going on, nothing to worry about, and that he was standing in front of a Jr. Mart and thought he'd be over right away and fill me in on the whole deal. Then he hung up before I could say I'd be looking for him, which is what I'd planned to say.

Judy always said she picked Ray out in a Dallas bar and married him for reasons unknown. "Because he's the furry type," she said. This was a joke between them, though Ray was furry—hair, beard, even his back that you saw when you went swimming with him, which I did once, a couple of years ago. The problem, according to her, was that he was "beady," too, around the eyes. "That'll kill you," she said. "Beady and furry. It's a bad combo."

I always wondered why he didn't get treatment for one or the other. Anyway, he still didn't have a steady job, he watched a lot of movies on TV, and, to hear Judy tell it, which Lily did in weekly phone calls, he wasn't a lot of fun to live with on a day-to-day basis.

It took him less than twenty minutes to make my back door. He was happy to see me, gave me a big smile, which made me feel lousy for the way I'd thought about him in the meantime.

"How-dee," he said when I opened the door. He slapped me on the shoulder, then held his hand there, pushing so I'd get out of the way and let him and his bag, which was like a small futon, into my kitchen.

I got out of the way. "Come on in." I slapped his back a couple of times. "Hey! You're a wet boy, aren't you?"

He grinned. "I'm Mr. Wet—where's Lil?"

He'd started calling Lily Lil, Diamond Lil, sometimes. It was his invention, nobody else ever called her that. I said, "She's at a gas station on East Bilbo Ave. She's got car trouble."

"God Damn!" he said, making a face like you'd make if thirty people just died in the crash of a light plane at O'Hare, and you were watching it on CNN. You'd watch the live coverage with this face. "She told me she was coming over here, left me a message."

"She's cooking dinner for me tonight," I said.

He was squishing around the kitchen in soaked running shoes, gray with purple decorations, a brand I didn't know, and he was already at the cabinets. "So," he said, yanking a Ziploc bag of candy—M & M's, Tootsie Roll Pops, orange play-peanuts—out of the bread cabinet. "Hey! Jackpot!" He laughed and tested the bag to see if the Ziploc was working. It wasn't, so we got candy on the counter, candy on the floor. He bent to get the stuff on the floor and stepped on a Tootsie Roll Pop that splintered and shot out from under his shoe. "Oops!" he said.

"Hold on," I said. "Freeze. Don't move."

"No. Hell, I got it," he said, lifting the foot, spraying

brown candy crystals around. Right then the phone rang. He pointed at it. "Incoming," he said. "That's a pretty phone, too. That a decorator model?"

It was a yellow telephone. It came with the house, or something. I don't remember.

Lily was calling again, this time to tell me the car was O.K. "It was low on oil, a quart low. There wasn't any on the stick when he pulled it out the first time, so I figured I'd torched the sucker, but this guy says the new ones are all that way, I mean, a quart low and they show nothing between those two creases on the end of the stick—you know what I'm talking about?"

"Ray is here," I said.

"Ray Ray?"

"Yes," I said.

By this time he'd made it across the kitchen and captured the receiver. "Ray to tower, Ray to tower," he said. "Come in with a friend. What's shaking, Lil?"

He gave me a grin and a black-eye wink, then unwrapped a Tootsie Roll Pop he'd saved, a red one, and plopped it into his mouth as he talked. After a minute he put his hand over the mouthpiece and said, "I'm sorry about this mess here, Peter. Just let me say hello to my sis and I'll clean her right up." Then he screwed up his face as if thinking about that, jabbed a forefinger into the telephone mouthpiece, and said, "The mess, I mean. Not her."

I nodded my understanding and went for paper towels, listening to his end of the conversation.

"You're too worried all the time, Lil. You're off the boulevard, here. You got to stay low, flop around with the rest of us. Huh? Keep moving, stay in the shadows. Hey, but it's great to be here! I mean, I'm looking forward to sitting down with you, you know what I mean?" He gave me good front teeth, laughing at the joke he was making. "Like at the dinner table. Maybe you can whip up that chicken thing you do, know the one I'm talking? Oranges and everything. Brown sugar? Boy, I've been missing brown sugar."

He was undressing as he talked, dropping the coat, then the shirt. He got the shoes off and was unbuckling his belt when he started doing kisses into the phone and pointed at it with his free hand to ask if I wanted to talk more. I nodded and took back the phone while he got down to his shorts.

"Hi. It's me, again."

"Have we got a problem there?" she said.

"He looks great," I said. "Wet right now, and naked, but good. He has a hair attitude, but I can't really decipher it. The hair's wet—he looks like a pop star."

"Pop star?" Ray said. He pulled the sucker out of his mouth and yelled, "We got designer hair. We got seventy-five bucks into the game right now." He pointed the red Tootsie ball at his head. "The latest," he yelled, leaning so close to the phone that I could smell his breath. "The hair's hot!"

"It's hot," I said to Lily.

"I weep for chicken!" he yelled.

. . .

When Lily arrived an hour later Ray was on the couch in a pair of tennis shorts and a red polo shirt reading my movies-on-TV book. He was smoking a thin cigar with a wooden mouthpiece, and talking out loud. "*Mr. Arkadin,*" he said. "A must-see—you ever seen that one, Lil?"

She went right by him, dripping, into the kitchen, where she started unpacking groceries. "Yep," she called, over the crackling bags. "It opens with an unmanned aircraft circling a foreign capital, right? There's a lot of stucco in it."

Ray dropped the book, swiveled off the sofa, and trailed into the kitchen. "You get me a surprise?" he said.

"Chicken," she said.

He did a quick circle, jamming both fists into the air one after the other, then danced around the room in a football-style frenzy—Martha Graham via Tone Loc. "I kill the chicken," he chanted. "I eat the wings, I break the back, ya ya!"

Lily was pleased. She had on jeans and sneakers and a heavy cotton sweater—all re-rumpled by the weather.

"And that's not all," she said, pulling a package of Malomars out of a sack. She did a flourish with the cookies, then spun them onto the countertop next to Ray. "For the Malomar man. You ate a hundred of these in one night, didn't you?" She turned to me. "Didn't Judy tell us he ate a hundred of these one time? They were fighting or something? Remember?"

I shrugged, although I did remember and I don't know why I didn't just say yes.

Ray groaned and rubbed his stomach. "God, I was crazy then. I must've been nuts. She was killing me about something or other, and then did the dinner thing, you know—" he did a mincing imitation of Judy that made her look like a bad TV homosexual. "Like what did I want for dinner right in the middle of this huge brawl we were having, and I said I wanted Malomars and went out to the store and bought about twenty packages and brought 'em back and dumped 'em all out on the table and sat there eating all night while she punched around on a salad with a tiny fork. Next day she told me I had the stink of the Malomar about me."

"You were looking for trouble," Lily said.

He grinned at her, something that was supposed to be conspiratorial, I guess, and said, "Still am." He must've thought the look I gave him was disapproving or something, because then he laughed and said, "Not really, Peter. I just said that to be interesting. Lil understands, don't you, Lil?"

She was busy working on the chicken, her back to us. "Sure," she said. "You're just talking, right?"

"Right," Ray said. "I'm a big talker."

"That's what we hear," Lily said. She has a way of saying things like that and making them seem, if not friendly, at least not terribly hostile.

I smiled at Ray, and he smiled back, the same smile as before, untouched. "Well," he said to me. "I suppose we're all wondering what I'm doing in these parts." He took out a new cigar and lit up, rolling the thing between his fingers while he mouthed the smoke. In a minute he let it out and said, "That's a good question. I'm glad you asked me that, Peter. Honest."

.   .   .

He didn't get a chance to tell us then because the doorbell rang. I went to get it and it was Judy, standing on the stoop looking like she'd walked over. She had on this huge coat, one of those thick, tan, winter jobs, good around Christmastime, and it was soaked, and her hair looked as if they'd just finished skull surgery on her and were trying to obscure the evidence. I hugged her, but then we got in the middle of this hug and she wouldn't let go, so I stood there looking at the rain falling off the edge of the roof and thinking that I'd probably like to hug her more if she weren't soaking wet. I felt guilty for thinking that, and for wishing she and Ray would just stay over at their house and have their fights alone, like everybody else, and then she said, "I love you, Peter. I really love you."

"Ditto," I said, thinking how uncomfortable it was when somebody says they love you and you're not expecting it, or when you take it for granted and wish they would, too. "Ray's here," I said. I was trying to wedge my way out of the hug, but she was having none of it.

"Oh, Christ," Judy said, and she started crying. It was a very quiet crying, she wasn't bawling, just standing there with her arms locked around me jerking like a mechanical device taking leave of its senses. I was trying to figure how to play the thing. Nobody'd told me anything—I mean, I knew there was a fight going on, but that's all. I was wondering what to do next when Lily came out of the kitchen with her fist inside of a three-and-a-half-pound fryer.

She said, "Who is it, Peter?"

"It's Judy," I said.

Ray stuck his head out of the kitchen. "Why, how-dee, Little Flower. How you doing? You following me around the country or something?" He moved across the foyer toward us as if to kiss her, but she was still hugging me and he pulled up short. "Oh," he said. "I forgot. We're having a wrangle, right?"

Judy nodded at him, splashing her hair around. "We were. That was last week sometime. Before you left without telling anybody in the world where you were going or anything."

"I slipped down to Tampa," he said. "I was looking

around. Checking it out. I was down there with Bruce Davis."

She looked at him, a steady look, then rolled her eyes toward the ceiling. "O.K. I give up. Who's that?" she said.

"TV guy," Lily said. "This ratty guy on a show." She waved the chicken at me and tried to change the subject. "We were in Tampa once."

"Only he ain't ratty," Ray said. "He looks like about a zillion. He had shoes on I'd be happy to drive around in. Had this jacket must've dropped him two thousand. Genuine chrome thread in there. Really."

"Ray hungers for the high life," Judy said. She'd finally let me go and had started hugging Lily, who could only hug back one-handed because of the chicken. You could tell it was bothering her. First she tried keeping it behind her back, then she tried a two-handed hug using just the arm of her chicken-hand, but that didn't work either, so the chicken was dangling out there at the end of her arm, there at her side, as she hugged Judy.

"That ain't it," Ray said. He was scratching his stomach again. "The guy looks like a Swiss, know what I'm saying? Like they scrub him with white bricks every morning. I asked the desk girl what he was doing there and she said she didn't know, but that she didn't think he was *shooting*, like I'm some kind of rube's gonna get in the way if the man's there *shooting*, know what I mean?"

"He didn't like the desk girl," Judy said.

I was worried about Lily and the chicken, so I put an arm around Judy and gave her a tug, trying to break up the thing, and I said, "Well, it's like old home week around here. I don't think I've had this many people in here since I got the place." I did another tug, this time toward the kitchen, figuring that even if I couldn't get them apart, at least in the kitchen Lily would have a chance on the bird. There were a couple of spots of watery blood on the tile there in the foyer, but it wasn't too bad.

Judy took this opportunity to start hugging me again. She got me around the neck with one arm so she wouldn't have to let go of Lily.

"Hell," Ray said. "This desk girl was main line, only she was main line Tampa, which is like a gum-wrapper town outside of Reno. Anyway"—he was keeping his distance, looking at the molding around the opening between the den and foyer—"there ain't anything there over four feet tall, know what I mean?"

"No, Ray," Judy said. "We don't know what you mean. Nobody ever knows what you mean." She finally gave up on Lily, though she still had me, and she pulled me over to the front door so we could get her shiny black duffel bag in off the stoop. This bag said "Players," like the cigarette, on the side. "Cars are taller than four feet, right?" she said when we got the door shut. "Don't they have cars in Tampa?"

"Sure," Ray said. "They got one. But it's this truck George Barris worked over in the fifties. Three foot eight."

She gave him an impatient smile.

"What I mean is," Ray started to say, but as soon as he started she waved him off, which gave me a chance to get free, so I did.

"We don't care," she said, looking at me. "I don't care, anyway." She pointed to Lily and me. "Maybe they care, but I don't care what you mean. You could mean anything in the world and I wouldn't care." She shouldered the wet Players bag. "I had to wear this coat because I don't have the right coat to wear at this time of the year in the rain because my husband's not such a knockout provider, if you know what I mean."

"Hey! I bought the coat," Ray said, talking to me and Lily, who had backed up all the way to the kitchen door.

"Yeah," Judy said. "My wedding present."

"There she goes," he said. "She's starting."

"Let me get this chicken put away," Lily said, waving the chicken-hand at me. "Why don't you get Judy settled and then we'll all meet in the kitchen for a drink."

"She doesn't drink anymore," Ray said. "She's into health. If it doesn't have spinach in it she won't touch it."

"I know this great spinach drink," I said.

All three of them shook heads at me. I shrugged and grabbed Judy's bag. "Let's go, dearest," I said. "We'll put you in the bedroom."

"Hang on," Ray said. "That's not my bedroom, is it?"

"I've got just the spot for you," I said.

"So what about my stuff?" he said. "I got it in the bedroom already. You gonna put her stuff in there with my stuff?"

Lily, who had gone around the corner into the kitchen and who had the water running in the sink, came back out drying her hands on three feet of paper towel and said, "So what's the deal? The luggage doesn't get along either?"

. . .

After dinner we sat around the rickety table and stared off in different directions, the four of us like people in one of those realistic sculpture setups you used to see in *Time* stories on modern art. Ray was watching something out the window over the sink. Judy was playing with blueberries in a bowl in front of her. Lily was reading the ads in the back of a boat magazine, and I was staring at the three of them, each in turn. We'd finished and we were just sitting there.

Judy said, "Where do these things come from, blueberries? I mean, where do they grow?"

"What are you talking about?" Ray said. "They grow on trees. Blueberry trees."

"Bushes," Lily said, without looking up.

"You mean what state?" I said.

"No," Judy said. "I meant how. I mean, I've never seen a blueberry grow."

"Oh, that's great," Ray said. "Spent all your time watching watermelons, did you?"

"I've got it," Lily said. She circled a spot on the magazine page with a pink marker. "This is it—twenty-eight-foot Bayliner. Cheap."

"That's your K mart, Lil," Ray said. "You'll be wanting a Bertram, be my guess. You can really hump a Bertram."

Judy said, "I'm sure that's just what she wants to do, Ray."

"La la la," Ray said.

"Why don't you leave her alone," Judy said. "If that's what she wants, that's what she wants."

"Oh, sure," Ray said. "Listen to Miss Genuine Fur-lined Downy-Soft They-Said-So-On-TV the Third." He was checking the skin on his arms, twisting his arms forward and pulling the skin around his biceps. "Do people get warts at my age? I've been finding splotches." He turned around to show me what he was talking about. "See that?" he said. "That look like a wart in embryo?"

There wasn't anything there—a sun dot or something. I said, "Doesn't look bad to me."

"May this house be safe from warts," Judy said, making an ugly face at Ray. "He's worried about his age. He's going to be forty-four this year and he's getting all these tiny age spots. They're everywhere, they're all over him."

"She's happy about it," he said.

"I don't know what's wrong with it," Judy said. "Your life's half over. So what?"

He dropped his face into one hand, covering his closed eyes with fingers and shaking his head. "I was forced to marry her, wasn't I?" He jerked up and smiled at me. "Oh, she's a wonderful woman, but it's a personality thing. She wants me to be a Ninja."

Judy did a too-bland-to-be-believed look. "That's a joke about me watching karate movies on TV."

"What the hell is a Ninja, anyway?" Lily said. "I've been hearing Ninja-this and Ninja-that for years and I've got no clue. They wear a lot of black, right?"

"At least Peter doesn't whine all the damn time because he's not Stevie Ray Vaughn or somebody. And he can keep a job," Judy said. "He has a career. He has a house—two of them, now. And he's only forty-something." She turned to me. "What are you now, Peter? Forty-six?"

"Not even close," I said. "Thanks."

"He's steady," Judy said. "That's what it's about."

Ray got up, adjusting the shorts again. "I know that it is," he said. "You're right. And it's a real nice house, too. Both of them, but this one especially. I wish it was my house. I wish I'd been living here the last five years."

.   .   .

An hour later I was lying in bed twitching the way I do when sleep won't come and my legs go numb—circulation stops and I jerk around like a kid getting electrocuted, or what we thought electrocuted would look like before we saw it on TV. It drives Lily crazy when I do it, so I got out of bed and went to the kitchen and had Rice Chex. I was sitting there thinking about Ray and Judy and how much trouble they were having and I started thinking about me and Lily, and how we got along pretty well. I mean, I started wondering if we were from another planet or something.

Then Judy and Ray came in. He was wearing an old robe of mine; she was still dressed. They were holding hands.

I looked at the clock on the stove but couldn't read it, which is something I hate. It happens all the time. Even in broad daylight the thing is hard to read. I said, "What time is it there?" and motioned toward the stove.

Judy bent over. "How do you read this thing?" she said. "Looks like it's four in the morning."

"It doesn't look like morning," Ray said. "Where does it say morning?"

She gave him a playful shove. "He's a detail guy," she said to me. "You know what I mean, right?"

"Twelve-twenty," I said.

Judy came over to the table and rubbed my shoulder. "We just want to apologize, O.K.? We're sorry to be messes, aren't we, Ray?"

"Yep," he said. He got a hand on my shoulder too.

They were both standing there beside me with hands on my shoulder, and I was sitting there wishing I'd stayed in the bedroom with Lily, thinking I should have been smart enough to stay out of the kitchen. "Nothing to worry about," I said, and I made as if to get up, thinking that'd get rid of the hands, at least.

It didn't work. Ray came with me to the refrigerator, kneading my shoulder on the way. "You know how these things go," he said.

Well, I did know, but what I was thinking was how much I hated it when people who have no business touching you go around touching you. I figured I couldn't say that without hurting his feelings, so I let it go and opened the refrigerator, thinking the sight of leftovers might encourage him to forget my shoulder and go for the food.

"We got it all worked out in the bedroom," Judy said, coming up behind us. "We're going back to our place now."

"Tonight? You don't want to just sleep over?" I couldn't even get close to sounding genuine. I hated that. I felt like a bad guy, like no brother-in-law at all. I reached into the refrigerator and got the black banana I'd been meaning to take out of there for a couple of weeks and handed it to Ray. "Toss this, will you?" I said. "It's Lily's, she brought it over here a month ago, but she'll never get rid of it. She loves that banana like a son."

"What's wrong with it?" Ray said. He held up the banana, twisting it back and forth as if trying to find the flaw.

"Hell, it's perfect," Judy said, slapping his back.

I said, "There's steak here if you want steak."

Ray said, "Steak?"

"No thanks," Judy said, poking his shoulder. "We'd better go. It's just that we wanted to come in and apologize for hanging you up with our troubles. We always do it, don't we?" She backed up to the counter opposite the refrigerator and hoisted herself up on the countertop. "I didn't want you to worry about me."

"She thinks you spend all your time worrying about her," Ray said. He had the banana stripped down and half-gone.

"I'm his friend," Judy said. "Of course he worries, don't you, Peter?"

"Sure." I was looking on the bottom shelf in the refrigerator at a Ziploc of black beans, trying to remember when I'd last had black beans. It seemed to me that it had been a while.

19

Ray and Judy decided not to go back to their apartment after all. The weather was too iffy and they were tired, Judy said, and Ray said they'd just hang around if it was O.K. with me. "Besides," he said, "if you're giving up this place maybe we can do a deal on the lease. Maybe we can talk about it tomorrow, O.K.?"

I said, "If tomorrow ever comes we can talk about whatever you like."

"You're not fond of Ol' Ray, are you?" Ray said.

"Sure I am," I said. "I'm just having a mood swing. I like you plenty. I think you're interesting."

"You do?"

"What's interesting about him?" Judy said. "Tell me quick."

"Pretty much every single thing about him," I said. "From head to toe. He's as interesting as the day is long."

"See that?" she said to Ray. "He can't name a single thing about you that's interesting."

"Thanks, Judy," he said.

We shook hands about something, anxiety I guess, and

then I left them and went to my bedroom to see how Lily was. It was the only time she'd slept over in this leased house and I was nervous. I don't know what I thought was going to happen to her, but I felt I needed to protect her, guard her, something like that. Maybe it was that I was afraid she'd leave without me, just go home, and nothing would have changed.

Lily was fine; she was asleep. I straightened the sheets and tried to get her to put her leg back under the top one, but she was having none of that, so I backed off, watched for a second, then went back out and down the hall into the third bedroom where I had a lot of boxes already packed for the move home, some full, some half-full. This room was too ugly for anything other than storage, too ugly to even sit in during daylight. A lot of the furniture that had come with the house, and that I hadn't moved into the garage, was shoved in there. The walls were paneled a milky off-white, a synthetic-wood version of bleached walnut, paneling you don't see that much except in the office parts of warehouses. There was an add-on half-bath in back and a sliding door opening to the patio, which was a pinkish slab that skirted the rear of the house then hit the driveway by the garage. The drapes in the bedroom were heavy, textured, moss-green, with torn places showing the water-stained backing. They looked tired of hanging there all the time. I sat down in the recliner and thought about getting wound up in trivial junk and how it had screwed Lily and me, thought about what we withheld from each other, what we hid, and why, and what we hoped to gain. I thought about how hard it was for any two people to maintain some fragment of decency and kindness toward each other, and how I'd messed that up with Dorothy, even though I hadn't gone crazy over her, I'd just slept with her.

Rain was coming and going. It was a thunder and lightning parade, seeming to grow closer, then to move away, then to come closer again. The lightning was dull and scattered, flashing the curtains Frankenstein-style.

I was going to try to sleep when I heard something outside that sounded like the scrape of an aluminum lawn chair on the patio. Just a clink sound, nothing you'd even hear, usually, only I got edgy at the slightest sound at night. Sometimes I'd hear a thump against a window, or a peculiar whine, or a sound like the cracking of twigs underfoot, and for weeks after I'd sleep with a two-pound, five-battery, metal-cased flashlight right alongside the bed. This was a legacy of my childhood when my parents were too far away in the house so that I never finally felt protected by them, not at night, not when I was alone and was sent to sleep. So I was put on edge by hearing this noise, and I looked around for a weapon, something heavy I could swing if necessary.

The portable phone was the only thing handy, so I grabbed that and eased out of the chair toward the window. Everything in the room was concert volume, every creak was ripping up the eardrums, the snap of my skin coming off the plastic seat was like a monster backbeat. I tried to find a hole in the curtain I could see through. There was what looked like an icepick puncture, but I couldn't see anything through it, so I got to the side of the sliding door and slowly pulled back the drapes. I got the window frame and an ant going down, then the glass, white with that caked dust that always collects at the edges of windows.

Outside, at the far end of the patio two people were kneeling together somehow on the concrete, one over the other. It didn't take a second to figure—they were fucking, or getting ready to. Another beat and I knew it was Ray and Judy; he was on the bottom, on his back, and she was kneeling above him, her pale butt clearly visible as she rubbed against him. Her shirt was out and open, off one shoulder, and her skirt was wrapped up at her waist; he had on that robe of mine, tied at the stomach, but the belt was the only part of it still around him. In a minute she was up, horseback-style, her trunk twisting in slow motion, tightening and releasing, then reversing left for right, like fabric caught in screw threads, she was turning, folding, scooping him up into herself, calibrating and pacing him, step by step; his hands were at her breasts, pushing, pinching, fanning against them, squeezing as if they were binoculars, until she caught his wrists, underhand, and moved his hands to her butt where she wanted him to hold her, to help her. Her back arched and it looked for a minute like she was trying to write her name with her hips, and then she was curved over him again, hands and knees, her hair tumbling in his face, her body almost motionless.

I was surprised. I didn't act quickly. I wasn't sure what to do. I figured I ought to quit watching but I wasn't doing that, quitting, I was just standing there, and then I was thinking about Lily, about maybe going to get her, but then I thought it was her brother and she wasn't going to want to see him like that, and then I realized I'd spaced-out, my focus drifted to a glittering yard lamp reflected in a streak of standing water along the driveway edge, behind them, over Judy's bare back. The picture was hazy, scattered, there was water on the glass, water dripping, the sky was busting a little with cloud-hidden lightning. I was cold, suddenly; I smelled the spoiled scent of the drapes I was holding; I wished fervently that none of this had happened.

I let the curtains fall back into place and I stood there alongside the window with my forehead pressed into the wall. I thought about yanking the door and yelling, "Hey! Cut it out!" or something like that, about getting into the den and clicking on the patio light, but I didn't do either of those things. Instead, I stood there listening to Ray and Judy, listening as carefully as I could.

I was thinking I'd missed Lily, that it was better to go through the day with her than without her, that it was peculiar how I loved her completely but not desperately, how I wanted her with me but could live without her, how I loved her touch but was mostly satisfied to hold her hand, to brush a hair from her cheek, to feel the curve of her waist as we stood at a window together. It was scary that we hadn't found a comfortable replacement sex for the middle age of our relationship. Scary how cool we were toward each other most of the time, how much of our love was reassurance and how little sex—it left me suspicious of the way I loved her, the cleanness of it, that so much was only longing, adolescent, frightened-of-loss longing, that it was so simple and childlike, such a precious feeling that I maintained and doubted myself for maintaining, a picture-book love.

But I loved loving her that way. What I hated was the suspicion, the doubt. That added to my anger and bitterness about what I was *supposed* to feel, how things were *supposed* to be.

But something was changing in me. I felt different, less angry, less willing to be angry. When I hated a guy at the office for lying, or somebody on TV for a specious argument, or a politician for unscrupulous ads, or a magazine article riddled with manipulative distortions, I hated less vigorously, the fire was down, maybe because I'd somehow sort of faced the hating, the resentment, by leaving home for a while, by disturbing the peace of our relationship, by risking it. Or maybe I was just capitulating, giving in, going over to the other side. I couldn't say for sure, but either way I suddenly had this new outlook: I could let other people alone, let them do what they wanted to do without comment. In spite of what they did or thought, or what I thought, I felt as if I could finally just leave them to their ideas and opinions, I didn't have to struggle to get them to do what I thought was right, or just, or fair, or interesting, it wasn't my responsibility to teach everyone, to fight for every single thing I believed in every minute of every day.

I figured other people learned this at sixteen, but for me it was a breakthrough at forty. Something had snapped, something new had happened, and if I now noticed that we were motivated by envy, covetousness, and avarice, if I noticed that we cloaked our most brutal behavior in our best rhetoric, if I noticed that we pretended to be on the highest of high roads at the instant of maximum baseness, I could let it pass without remark. Why? Who knew? Maybe I was too tired to argue or complain. Maybe I knew I wouldn't win. Maybe it didn't matter if I did. Maybe I'd mistaken getting older for something it wasn't. Maybe I'd forgotten the lessons you learn at twenty. Maybe I'd realized that bitterness, resentment, brutality, cruelty, depression, aimlessness, loneliness, rage, fear, and all the other distresses were real and present in each of our lives equally and without exception, period. Maybe it was knowing all our terrors are the same, though their details are endlessly different. Maybe it was none of that, just an accident, a trick of pure feeling.

.   .   .

"What's the deal?" It was Lily, out of bed, standing beside me in the back bedroom, bumping her head into the side of my arm. "What are you doing back here? Did you hear something? Is something outside?"

I still had the phone-weapon in my hand. I smelled her hair and I thought for a minute about not saying anything, about turning her right back toward the bedroom. Then I said, "No, it's just Ray and Judy."

"Oh, yeah?" She leaned back and looked at me, squinting. "What are they doing? Are they outside? What time is it?"

"Late," I said. "They appear to be making love. I think they're making love."

It was like Lily was suddenly awake. "What? Is this a joke or something? Get outta here." She stepped around me, reaching for the curtain.

I caught her arm. "I'm serious," I said.

She took the curtain with her free hand and pulled it a good foot away from the window's edge. "Shit," she said.

I looked, too. Ray and Judy had swapped positions and they were going after each other. It wasn't exciting to watch this, it was like porn when you aren't interested—too clear, too true.

"I don't believe this," Lily said. "Suddenly it's Bombay."

"I think they made up earlier," I said. "I mean, I talked to them and they had worked out whatever it was they needed to work out."

"I'm glad for them," she said, turning away from the glass. "But I don't know why this has to go on here. I mean, what's this mean? What's this about?"

"I think this is more of the same," I said. "The world as we know it down around our ears."

"It's been there a while already, hasn't it? I thought we all agreed that Ralph was a scum hog for doing just this sort of thing at the party—didn't we agree that?"

"I think we're supposed to be asleep, to look away," I said. "And, yes. We agreed something like that but not exactly. In the first place Ralph isn't your brother. In the second place, Ralph was just noodling around, whereas this here appears to be the real thing." I pointed at the curtain. "You about finished with that? Want to close her up?"

Lily let go of the drapes. "For some people things never change," she said, heading for the recliner. "Ray is going to be this way until he dies."

"A while ago it was us, wasn't it? And in daylight."

"Sure, but we weren't being watched. There was nobody here to watch us."

"Neighbors," I said. "Besides, does that mean it didn't happen?"

"Never mind," Lily said. "I didn't mean anything. I never mean anything. I try as hard as I can not to *mean*. It's not a thing I like to do. You try to mean and then you're wrong, that's the basic equation in life as far as I'm concerned. I prefer to *do* instead. They can't take it away from you, and no matter how hard they try they can never finally know what you *mean* by what you *do*. Even if you tell them they don't know."

"What's all this?" I said. "Who's they?"

"It's an extended other, like in self and other. A debased concept, I guess."

"But time honored," I said.

I was moving around the room, shifting boxes here and there, scraping my heels on the floor, making as much noise as I could. Lily watched me for a minute, then broke into a quiet laugh, mouth closed, air shuttling through her nose, her shoulders doing slight contractions. She said, "It's O.K., Peter. I've heard it before. You don't have to make white noise. Come here, will you?"

I dropped the box I was relocating and moved toward her sliding my feet ski-style for the big noise—a joke. She held up her hand and I took it, sat on the arm of the chair beside her, almost tipped myself in. "So?" I said.

"So are we getting together again?" Lily said.

"I think so, yes," I said. Then we just sat there for a couple of minutes and thought about that, about what that meant, what it might mean, how it felt that that's what we were doing. It felt good, as good as anything had for a while. I said, "And if our friends ever finish we're next for the patio."

"*Mon dieu!*" Lily said. "Can this be so? Could this be magic?"

She held her palm against my cheek. Her hand was cool, dry, very light on my face. I turned so the edge of her first finger slipped between my lips, opening my mouth, resting against my teeth. There was no taste to the finger, only the pressure and the clean scent of her skin.

. . .

Lily and I were napping in the recliner together when I heard a noise and jumped up, and the jumping woke her. Ray was standing in the door to the hallway clicking a fingernail against the hardwood door frame. "You guys going to sleep like that?" he asked. "I think you'll be sorry if you do. I saw the bedroom door open and nobody in there so I wondered where you were."

"We were just resting," I said. "We were talking and we must've fallen asleep."

I didn't know if he realized we'd watched him, but then

I saw him figure it out, I saw his face change. "Uh," he said, looking at his sister, then at the drapes. He reached for the edge of the drapes and pulled them back, looking outside. "This is a window? I guess it is, huh? Right out onto the patio, Jesus."

Lily got out of the chair and crossed the room. She took his hand and changed the subject. "So Peter tells me you guys made up and everything. That's good."

"If you can do it, we can do it," he said. "We're even thinking of buying a house. The problem is you buy one and that eliminates all the others."

"A classic problem," she said. "Like marriage, divorce notwithstanding."

Judy came up behind Ray, stopped a minute, then came into the room and took over the recliner. I don't know why we stayed there, why we didn't go back into the living room, or the kitchen. I guess we were stuck together there. The rain had come back, light, pattering rain that barely sounded when it hit the roof, the leaves outside, the already wet patio.

Judy was obviously uncomfortable, a bright smile shooting into place every time one of us glanced her way. "Can I ask you guys a bonehead question?" she said. "I've been thinking that we probably ought to try to do something more serious, like, with our lives. I mean, I'd like to."

"What's serious?" Ray said. "Sting? Is Sting serious? I guess so, I mean, he's on the rain forest case, isn't he. Or what about that guy in the paper who never gives up yuppie bashing, what's his name? It's like he's named after a toilet water or something? Is he serious? He acts awfully serious. Or maybe we ought to do something to dramatize once again how the poor are mistreated by the rich—that'd be serious. But you'd think we'd have had our fill of that story by now, wouldn't you?"

"Oh God," Lily said. "He's getting the Peter disease."

Judy said, "What about terrorism, hunger, duplicity, fanaticism, racism, child abuse, animal experimentation, drugs, greed, abuse of power—those are some of the ones I've been thinking about."

"Right," Ray said. "You're not one of these fodder-queens who believes that saying you're doing something is the same thing as doing it, are you? A social scientist? You want to give me a clue how we're going to straighten out that stuff?"

She burnished her feet against each other for a minute, then propped them on the footrest. "I don't know what you mean. I guess we could join something. Call somebody. How does anybody influence those things?"

"Hey! Great question!" Ray said. "Maybe they don't. Maybe they just talk all the time and don't get anything done."

"That's always been your idea," Lily said. "Random junk. Nobody believes that anymore."

"I don't care," Ray said. "Doing stuff like that is a sinkhole. You start out with good intentions and end up believing your own PR. Then your whole world is squad commanders in the anti-terrorism unit, crash investigators, policy mavens, corporate watchdogs, and everything's a re-warding and high-paying career opportunity with quick-learn certification, immediate advancement, a big social pro-file and the public conscience to match."

"I think that's silly, Raymond," Judy said. "I'm sorry I even asked you anything about it."

"You may be sorry, but you're still responsible," he

said. "Peter, have you got any salt in here? This needs salt." He was pointing to a glistening gray-white slug that had inched into the room under the curtains.

I went into the bathroom and came back with three Wendy's salt packets.

"Thanks," he said. "See, first you've got to get somebody to agree with you. You see a problem, they've got to see it. Then you've got to agree on what to do. The only people who agree are the ones paid to agree. And if you try to start small, to do something right at your office, or in your neighborhood, you find out that what people want is to replicate themselves. Period. People who wear suits think everybody should wear suits; people who never wear suits think nobody should ever wear a suit. The same for politics, religion, and sports. These are the great areas of interest in America today, the third being more profoundly interesting than the other two by far."

"And hair," I said. "Don't forget hair."

"O.K.," Ray said, shaking the salt packets. "Four great areas of interest."

"Don't put salt on that thing, please," Lily said. "It'll squirm around and everything. Please, Ray."

Judy got up and took the salt packets away from him. "Hey, he's a cynical guy, eh?"

"They teach it on MTV," he said. "That's the best of it."

"O.K.," Lily said, breaking a yawn with her fist. "Enough. Ray is on record as preferring truth and beauty. At any cost, I presume?"

"I guess it sounds pretty idealistic, doesn't it?" he said.

"You're nuts, Ray," Judy said. "That's the problem. You're not giving anybody a chance at all."

"No, I'm not," he said. "What's going on is grim and

insidious, and it's getting worse. The root is dishonesty, the particular strain is covetous hedonism masquerading as morality, the mechanism by which it works is self-righteousness."

"I don't want Peter hearing any of this," Lily said.

"I heard, already," I said.

"And we're so disenfranchised we don't even know we're disenfranchised, we think we're in the show," Judy said. She was parodying Ray, talking mechanically. "The culture is falling apart faster than it's mending. The falling apart factors in social changes that underwrite the continued failure." She gave Ray a nasty little grin. "I've heard this part a hundred times."

"Have they got it figured out or what?"

"So who's our model of correct cultural and behavioral standards?" Lily said.

"Nobody," he said. "The options are chivalrous anarchy or secular Christianity—do unto others, that sort of thing. The rest is shit-rubber bullets and death cults and drug assassinations and political witch-hunts. If people get hurt say you're sorry and blame the victim."

"We're all-world in the evil department," Judy said. "That's the idea. If it seems too simple—"

"We're ordinary," he said. "What's missing is the possibility of benevolence. We can't even imagine it anymore. So we do what everybody else does. Maybe we always did, I don't know. But now we can't even think of anything else, now it's just screw the other guy before he screws you. Ricky Nelson was right."

"Did Ricky say that?" I asked.

"I think so," Ray said.

20 We went back to bed, leaving Ray and Judy to find their way to Charles's room, where they were supposed to be sleeping. Lily had taken my side of the bed, so I had the other side, the side I never sleep on, and that was uncomfortable. I was on Lily's side of the bed and she was on mine. I don't think she was too comfortable either. She was stretching and moving around trying to get settled for sleep, and after about ten minutes of that she sat up and said she wanted to go out.

I said, "No."

"C'mon," she said. "We haven't done it in a long time. We'll drive around and see stuff, you know, the beautiful world of the night and so on, we'll go to the Snack'O'Matic, we'll drag Main. C'mon, it's the middle of the night."

"Haven't we had enough interesting stuff for one day?" I said. "And we're old people, and it's raining, and it's foggy out there, and I'm not sure there's any gas, and we can't leave them here alone—they'll get into videotape or something and then we'll all end up at the police station."

"Hot dog," she said. "We can do a Rob Lowe look-

alike thing, we can do Seniors Snared in Video Sex Shack—
will you please stop with the old people?"

"I'm thinking I'm sixty-five, maybe more, but it's not
bad. I can think worse. The thirties, the twenties, the teens—
other than that it's been terrific."

Lily was out of bed, hopping around pulling on her
pants. "I'm going," she said. "Are you coming? I'm going
to show you stuff you've never seen before. We're going to
burn this town. I've got an all-night fish market in my head,
a train station, a lonely street in the rambunctious district,
I've got high wires and singing rivers and the long dark
shadows that ride in lime-colored light. I'm going to show
you stuff, scorching crazy stuff, ore ships on fire at the edge
of Orion—"

"Attack," I said. "In the movie they were attack ships."
I sat up in the bed.

"Right," she said. "Come on. Hustle it up there. You
want to go out the window or should we just sneak? They're
going to hear us if we sneak."

"That's O.K.," I said, sliding off the bed. "We *saw*
them."

"What if they want to come? That's not the deal. Are
we man enough to tell them they can't come?" She was
pulling a T-shirt over her head, one of mine, one that said
STOVETOP in six-inch upcase, two lines, four letters each, no
hyphens.

"We are," I said. "We can go toe-to-toe with them. We
can tell them whatever we want. We're the boss, we're the
one." By now I was alongside the bed in my bare feet. I
had jeans on and I was looking for a shirt that didn't feel
too used. I decided to get a fresh shirt. I went to the closet.

Lily said, "What're you, putting on a new shirt to go
out for a drive? Maybe I'd better dress a little more." She

held the bottom edge of the T-shirt, stretched it down in front of her, pressing the cotton against her chest, across her nipples.

"You're fine," I said. "You're a natural."

Then we creaked and snapped through the house. I was carrying my shoes. We were giggling because Lily made some joke about finding Ray and Judy in the backseat, thumping away. I told her she ought to slow down about it. I told her she was going to get the essay questions if she didn't watch out. You never can tell, I told her.

We went out the kitchen door, pulled the door to, but didn't lock it, got into her car. There was a faint ringing in my ears. The street lamps all looked as if they had star filters. There were fingered grease lines on the windshield. Everything outside was wet, covered with a thin layer of tiny bubbles, bubbled water, everything was glistening just like it always glistens during rain. Even the telephone wires shined. I felt chilly, like when fall starts feeling like fall, so I turned my collar up, buttoned my shirt all the way to the neck.

We rolled out of the driveway and smacked the empty garbage can, knocking it into the street. Lily stalled the car. I got out and tossed the can back up into the yard. In the car I ran my window down. I could hear bugs, crickets chattering. There was a loose breeze, slow and floating through the air, barely moving the bush limbs on people's lawns. She was going to restart the car, but I stopped her. I said, "Wait a minute. Roll your window. Listen."

She did and we sat in the road in the car, silent for a minute. When she brought her window down, another breeze eddied through. It was cold enough to make you shiver. It smelled like winter, like a long winter. It smelled like spring, too. It was odd out there, the breeze was odd. Even though we were close to the house the air carried this scent of being in the middle of nowhere, a scent I remembered from times at the beach, or at the bay, times at people's ranches when I was a kid. It was the smell of too much freedom, too much anything goes, too much anything can happen, of everything else is too far away. It's a great smell if you're seventeen and going to some girl's house after a Friday-night football game, or if you're eighteen and at a party at the beach with your high-school sweetheart, or if you're twenty-three and staying up all night partying at college. It's even great if you're twenty-nine and you've got a job and you've got a girlfriend and you're spending the week at somebody's condo in Florida and it's three in the morning and the wind is cutting in off the Gulf and you're walking in sand a foot deep, so thick you have to heel-and-toe-it down the beach. There are stars transmitting out there, and there's a moon, and the waves are slapping around. When you lose sight of the lights you suddenly feel extraordinarily isolated, separated, like no one could ever reach you. It's a feeling of power, and at the same time, tenderness, sadness. That's how the air in the car smelled—new, fragrant, damp, moving slowly but not stopping.

"Can I start the car now?" Lily said. "Have we finished our sitting-in-the-car experience?"

"Let her rip," I said.

The street was crowded with trees that hung over the pavement making a kind of tunnel, so the street lamp light was blotched and spotty. The tires sputtered on the concrete. I put my arm out the window, wetting the sleeve of my shirt in two places, below the shoulder, below the elbow.

Lily reached out and patted my thigh when we got to

the stop sign at the corner of my street. "Which way?" she said. She pointed left and then right and then left again, waiting for my answer.

"You're the chief," I said.

"Let's go out Fifty-nine," she said. "You want to?"

"Sure," I said.

. . .

So we cut down a couple of side streets, half-lit beaded concrete streets with shallow curbs, streets flanked on either side by nondescript tract houses from the fifties, brick houses from design books, doing better every day, until we ran dead-end into the feeder for the highway. At that point we were surrounded on all sides by bushes. You could see the pale bluish light over the rise that was directly in front of us, coming up behind the greenery, which was now dark and slick, the light sizzling over this thirty-foot slope. You couldn't see any of the cars moving up there, just this light, and this sound of the cars going by, the tires running on the wet concrete, the water strewn behind them. We had the windshield wipers going even though the rain was light and it took a few minutes for it to obscure the view. But we had them going, opening those messy arcs on the glass. There wasn't much to see. We turned right and drove on the feeder for a mile, maybe a little less. The hill we had run into gradually declined so that where the feeder finally offered us access to the freeway, we only had to go up ten or fifteen feet. At that point we could see the highway, the tall lamps with the fuzzy rain in front of them, the cars with their bursting lights, headlights and taillights, streaming by. The freeway wasn't all that crowded at that time of night, but it was eerily bright, lighted up almost as if it were day. Just after we got on the freeway we went under a cloverleaf.

There were four levels above us, and there was one below, dug out of the ground, going ninety degrees to our direction.

Lily said, "This is gorgeous, this is wonderful. This is worth living for." She reached over and rubbed my leg. It was a loving touch, it was a touch that said how much she cared about me, how she cared about me, and how glad she was that we were going to make it after all. I put my hand on the back of hers while hers was still on my leg, pressing my fingers between the tips of her fingers and then drawing my hand back, drawing my fingers back between her fingers, until my fingers rode up onto the back of her hand. I did that a couple of times, like I was raking her hand.

I thought I must feel just about the same way she did, just about as happy about the resolution of our situation as she was, I thought it was better than I deserved and not nearly as good as she deserved. I said, "It is kind of pretty out here, isn't it?"

Just at that point some guy in an old black Camaro with a cockeyed headlight and busted mufflers went by doing about seventy, throwing off a rooster tail that slapped against our windshield as if it had been shot from a fire hose. The water hit with a fierce splash and a sudden covering of the glass, so for a minute you couldn't see a thing out the front, you could only hear the hammering of the Camaro's exhaust like an automatic weapon, receding.

"Fucked you, didn't he?" Lily said, as the wipers got the glass clear. Then she watched me pull my arm in the window and try to wring out some of the water in the soaked sleeve of my shirt.

"He was a darling," I said. "He was not a black person or a Mexican-American person, however. He was not a woman, not anyone disadvantaged in any way. He was not from any minority group. He was not a member of any little-known or lesser-known religious community, not a homosexual, nor a holder of any minority beliefs, he was not a person psychologically or socially dysfunctional in any way, he had never been treated for any of the possible addictions. In short, he was one of us. Some asshole doing seventy in the rain. No wonder they hate us."

"He looked like a Mex to me," Lily said.

"No, it was a kid," I said. "Blond, laughing, crew-cut. One of the new American crew-cuts." I reached in the back seat for what I thought was a towel, but it turned out to be a bath mat, one of the furry nylon types. "What's this doing in here?"

She looked over to see what I was talking about. "Oh, I got it at a yard sale. I was coming home from work the other day and there was this big yard sale, and I stopped and got that bath mat. It's just a backup bath mat for the bath mat I already have. I thought I might need an extra bath mat sometime."

We were headed downtown on the loop that passed just on the other side of the new wish-I-was-designed-by-a-famous-architect convention center, and a huge truck carrying forty-foot lengths of pipe big enough for a person to live in swept by us on the left, in the lane closest to the median. The contrail off that truck shoved us half a lane over to the right. Then we went up an overpass to miss an intersection starring four brand-new convenience store service stations, then down into a ten-lane channel where we drove for a couple of miles beneath ground level. The concrete that made the sides of this road was washboard-fluted, leaning away from us as it rose to the streets above, rerouting the water with delicate fountainlike precision. Every couple of blocks there was a bridge across above us with a mean-looking fence topped with meaner-looking wire. The kids didn't worry about the wire; all the bridges were painted with slogans and graffiti, spray-can art. Skulls and cross-bones, transformer-types, hatchet-jaw profiles, huge knives dripping blood, swarthy-looking biker faces, backwards swastikas, and the familiar array of unintelligible shorthand. Above us, out of the trench, a searchlight was circling from somewhere, maybe from a building downtown. When it passed over us a veil of blue-white light slid across the hood, through the windshield, over Lily and me, and out the back. The lightning was still going off in the sky, but it was so far away you couldn't really see very much, it looked like something happening in another room, behind thick velvet curtains. If there was thunder I couldn't hear it over the sound hash of the cars running through the standing water on the freeway. I scanned the dashboard, checking gas, tem-perature, speed, time—it was one-forty-seven. The radio wasn't on, but its controls were lit up with orange blocks of light, faint orange numbers on shallow push buttons.

The Camaro showed up again, coming from behind and hugging the inside island. He hung back a minute, riding alongside of us with the front of his car about even with our front seat, before going past. He had his windows down. I caught the image of his face, lit from his dash and the reflected highway lamps, and he looked pleasant enough, he looked like he was having a good time. I remembered myself at his age borrowing my father's car on some phony errand, out driving at night, nowhere to go, particularly, stopping in gas stations to use the phone when I'd think of someone to call, feeling bad when nobody was home, or nobody could get out, then driving again, on the local free-ways, alone, like this kid.

I said, "I thought this guy'd be in L.A. by now. He

must've gotten off and come back on." I pointed out the Camaro as it went by.

"Got him," she said, cranking her window up a couple turns.

"This drive used to be so beautiful it just tore me apart, just drove me crazy. I just wanted to be out here all the time, I wanted it to be like this all the time, but now it's different. I like it, but it's not irresistible."

Lily took a deep breath, smelling the rainy air that flooded the car. She rolled her window down again, looking around, left to right, out her window, out the windshield, out my window, ducking to see out the upper part of the windshield at the sky. "This stuff means the same thing to everybody," she said. "It's all about risk and possibility, it's about love, it's about hope, excitement. How else could they have turned it into advertising so quick?"

"It's a horrible new world," I said. "They needed another way to sell some shit so they took this little bit of real stuff away from us and put it on television, proving again that anything can be packaged and delivered at push of button; the problem is like the guy said about the postcard of the Grand Canyon: the TV version *becomes* the real thing." I swung my hand across in front of me, above the dashboard, at the glass. "I don't even know what this is out here now."

"Aren't you the guy who said we're supposed to love whatever's happening, that it doesn't matter what it is as long as we can be in love with it?"

"I used to be that guy," I said. "But I'm some other guy now. I'm doing something else. I'm not sure it's better. Maybe I'm trying to get back to that thing you're talking about. I mean, it's a great idea. It used to be that if something was odd it was wonderful, but I've seen so much odd shit now I'm sure that's not enough. It used to be oddness was about human frailty, the mistakes we make, the stupid things we do, the pathetic ways we try to cover our tracks, but now I'm less patient so I begin to think we shouldn't do so many stupid things, we shouldn't make so many mistakes, we shouldn't have to cover our tracks."

She gave me a look and a sideways smile and said, "This after six months, complaining about TV announcers?"

"It's a surprise, isn't it? Anyway, it wasn't them, it was that they define everything for the rest of us, and we let them. The axiom is define the turf, win the argument. Didn't somebody smart say that?"

She said, "It was somebody in the Middle Ages, probably. They were always saying stuff like that back then. Somebody in my dreams."

"It's like abortion, as soon as they get *your* fetus on the agenda you might as well trash your king."

"So that's what happened to you?" She turned for a second to see what I thought about that, then shrieked, cutting the wheel to the right quickly to avoid a pickup that veered into our lane. "Jesus!" she said, glancing over her right shoulder to be sure there weren't any cars in the lane we were crowding. "I wonder where's he's heading?"

"I don't know," I said. "He's probably with the other guy." The truck crossed in front of us and angled right two more lanes, then hugged the outside of the freeway. I saw a light click on in the cab, and it looked as if the guy was trying to read a map. "I'd stay out of his way," I said. "He doesn't know which way is up."

"Who does?" Lily said. "Never mind. I don't know what I'm talking about. A lot of times I say stuff and don't know why, but then it means something, I mean, it's about something, so it's O.K."

I felt punchy and fatigued, as if it were way past my

bedtime. Another clock up alongside the highway said two o'clock, then switched to the temperature. It was forty-eight. "And, yes. I got caught for a while. But I'm on the mend."

"Good," she said. "I was just checking."

After another couple of underpasses we went up a shallow grade and slanted to the left, eventually making a ninety-degree turn, and then we were in the middle of a six-story, twenty-lane switching corridor of a half-dozen different freeways. It was an amazing place, lots of high galvanized fencing, huge concrete columns, some twenty feet high, some sixty or more, holding up the top roads, and there were freeways crossing under other freeways, roads running parallel and then splitting off from one another, roads diving to the right or to the left to avoid connections with other highways, or diving to make connections, and at the bottom of the whole corridor a set of freshly painted lanes that formed the bed of this spooky place. I knew this part of the freeway, of course, we'd been through it a hundred times, five hundred times, but it never failed to stun me with its complexity, its grace, the danger of its intersections, the quirkiness of the linkages drivers routinely made, day after day, the quickness with which decisions came upon you. One moment you were on track, moving forward at freeway speeds, knowing exactly where you were and where you were going, where you were supposed to be in this elaborate set of intersections, and the next moment was a chaos of possibilities, of exits flashing by faster than you could figure which they were, where they went, of ramps cantilevered off in odd directions, of stacked and clustered signs pointing out connections to Interstate 59, 75, 31 East, 45 South Thru Traffic, 610 Loop, 45A Truck Route, and delivering instructions: SLOWER TRAFFIC RIGHT, LEFT LANE EXIT ONLY, THROUGH TRAFFIC CENTER LANES, ILLEGAL TO STOP IN

ROADWAY, STAY OFF MEDIAN, DO NOT CROSS, LEFT LANE CLOSED 3:30–7:00 P.M., NO SLOWING, CAUTION, LANE ENDS.

At two in the morning in this light feathered rain, cars slinging through this three miles of gigantic erector set multi-tiered auto-pinball sideshow, this paradise, we were all strange travelers, cars like bullets fired by chance at unknown targets. We would never know each other. Somebody went by two levels above the level we were on in a green DeSoto, it looked like a DeSoto, huge clouds of dirty smoke pouring out the back, the car just chugging across a curved descending spiral to get on the freeway headed west. Two trucks sailed by us on our right throwing up veils of water. Somebody coming at us flicked his brights on and off, then on again. On a high road crosswise to the one we were on there was a truck with a load of huge logs parked tight against the side of this forty-foot-high overpass. Two guys were standing in front of this truck, at the guardrail, looking down at us.

Suddenly we hit one of those points of decision and had to choose whether to go left on a narrow one-lane exit or to go straight, staying on the freeway we were on—our lane ended, turning into this exit. For some reason Lily wanted to take the left. "I'm going to go," she said. "I'm taking this one."

"No, no," I said. I reached over and tugged at the wheel, not hard enough to stop her if she really wanted to turn, but hard enough to indicate I didn't want to go that way.

"Let go," she said. "Quit fucking with the wheel. O.K., O.K. I'm not going. Let go."

I poked Lily's shoulder and pointed, and she glanced over, nodded, made a grunting sound.

We skipped two exits that would have taken us into

downtown, and then Lily pulled over to the right lane and slowed, bobbing her head up and down like one of those toy dogs with the spring-loaded necks you see in the back windows of cars; she was trying to read signs suspended above.

I said, "What are you looking for? Which way do you want to go?"

"I've got it," she said, swinging the car back toward the center lane. "I want to go out by the ship channel. I want to go out there in the industrial section where the air is pure chemical waste, nothing but toxic products off the big refineries; I want to go out there where the big flames shoot out of the tops of things. I like the huge lawns they put in front of their refineries. They've got the best lawns in town."

"So you want Fifty-nine North, is that it?"

"Hey," she said. "Joke. You with me here?"

"Sorry," I said. "I'm getting too earnest these days. I don't know what's happening to me."

"Maybe you were replaced. One of those pod things. Anyway, I'll get us there, don't worry. You just sit tight. Maybe we'll even go to the Greek dancing place. No, I guess that's a bad idea. But, remember that mound thing in Florida, in Tampa, where we went down this road and it was like the road from nowhere, lots of signs shaped like animals and palm trees, lots of bars and that place called the Low Slung Cafe, and there was this huge slope of earth, squared off, it must have been a mile long and a mile wide, fifteen stories high? Remember there was a car on top of it, way up there? And we couldn't even get in because it had some danger sign or something, and the next day, from that hotel room downtown I saw this thing from the top and it was filled with runoff from somewhere? Like it was a treatment thing. You remember all that? It's strange, huh?"

I rolled my head left against the headrest and stared at her, meaning to suggest how strange it was for her to remember this place we'd seen three or four years before, but she didn't turn around to meet my stare. I shrugged and looked at the windshield, at the door-swings the wipers were drawing on the glass. My mouth was dry. With all the highways above us and alongside of us and crossing over us and crossing beneath us, being in that panlike space under the other freeways, the water cutting down in some spots and being blocked in others by the roads above us, by the high strips of concrete and the columns and the twisting exits and the spirals of freeways joining other freeways, of freeways turning upon themselves, I felt splendidly safe and happy, like I was finally home, like I was where I belonged, someplace I could stay forever, and so I thought I ought to thank God for that and I made a small version of the sign of the cross on my lips with the nail of my thumb, a sign no bigger than a diamond, like a tiny, star-shaped incision.

.   .   .

Then the kid in the Camaro was back. He was on our left, his windows down. He pulled right beside us and matched speeds. He was soaked, his shirt was soaked, his short hair was matted tight to his head. At close range he wasn't a good-looking kid. He grinned at me when I caught him out of the corner of my eye, turned toward him and did a tight nod, then turned away.

Lily wasn't looking. "Hot Rod," I said to her, and I watched her huff, her rib cage contracting slightly.

Then, when she turned to look at him, right then the kid brought up a pistol from the seat beside him, a big gun, chromed, and he was waving it around, watching us and the road at turns, back and forth, steering the Camaro with his left hand cocked over the top of the wheel, the exhaust cracking loud like a truck.

We were near the end of this set of freeway exchanges, pulling out from under an overpass, the parallel highways above us peeling off up ahead, two to the left, one to the right.

Lily said, "He's kidding, right? Jesus, do you believe this?" She twisted quick toward me, then back toward the Camaro, rocking the steering wheel as she did, so that we swiveled a couple of feet each direction, slid a bit, then took hold again when she dropped off the gas.

The Camaro slowed, too. The kid made a waving motion with the gun, telling us to speed it up, not to slow down. He looked like Rutger Hauer, that's what struck me, what occurred to me, like a very young, thin-faced Rutger Hauer. He checked his rearview mirror, then added that to the cycle of what he was watching—mirror, road, us.

I swung around and looked out the back window hoping we had some traffic behind us, but there wasn't anybody there. No trucks, no cars, nothing.

"What do I do?" Lily said, facing ahead, her hands tight on the wheel, sitting up like a demonstration of proper driving posture.

"Fuck if I know," I said. "Get away from him. Move over here." I motioned right, keeping my hand low so he wouldn't see.

She twisted the wheel and edged us off to the right, putting a lane between us and the kid, but he followed right away, followed again when she started to go over another lane.

"Great idea," Lily said. "Really. What's next?"

The guy was pointing the gun at her and then at me, taking potshots like a kid with a cap pistol, pursing his lips as if doing the sound effects, jacking the gun barrel back and up after every shot, mimicking the recoil. I saw everything he did very clearly, I saw the expression on his face, saw his eyebrows arch each time he pretended to pull the trigger, saw his eyes flick back and forth from us, to his mirror, to the road. Saw him squint.

I said, "I don't know what he's doing. Just keep going. Maybe it's not a real gun. Keep driving."

"I can hit the brakes?" she said. "Never mind. Forget it. I don't think it's a good idea."

He was swinging his Camaro at us, slipping it over into our lane, pulling up close, swaggering with this car, but he didn't hit us. He came close but he didn't hit us. If he just tapped us it would be like a ship gets hit underwater in a movie—thunk, then we'd go flying. He had the pistol flat on the back of the seat, resting there. It was like this gun was too heavy for him to keep pointing it at us all the time. But it was in his hand, right there. There was lots of noise, water noise, muffler noise, engine noise, wind—all of it bouncing off the cars and the ramps and the concrete we were under, and there was that washy sound like you get when you drive out of a tunnel onto an open highway.

He pulled ahead of us for a minute and I thought he was finished, he was leaving. He rode up there and Lily started slowing, she got down to forty-five, forty, but he didn't pull away, just sat there on our left front fender, his taillights just ahead of us. We did that for a while, then he suddenly slid straight across the lanes in front of us from her side to mine, then back, quickly, abruptly, so Lily hit the brakes and pulled left, toward the median. She stopped there.

He stopped, too. He was ten feet away, a little in front, on my side.

Not moving in the middle of the freeway was eerie, like we were caught in a movie or something, like we were on a set, dark and shiny, the sound like the white noise of rain and distant tires split by his car radio playing some crazy music that didn't figure, some polka or something. We sat there a second not moving, taut in our seats. I was staring straight ahead, moving just eyes looking around. His car idled rough, loping and irregular. Something was whining in his engine, like a compressor belt, something screeching every couple seconds.

He had the gun over his left arm, pointing it again, and he made a move with his eyes telling us to get started. His head was tilted back against the headrest and twisted our way. "Go," he said. The voice was soft, and then he chuckled, did it again with his eyes, then with the gun, wagging us forward.

"O.K.," I said, looking from him to Lily.

"I'm going." She pressed the gas and we started moving again. "I'm not trying anything," she said.

We got back to freeway speed pretty quick, and the Camaro dropped back past me on the right side and pulled in behind us, flicking lights so we wouldn't get any ideas. The kid gunned his engine and jumped the Camaro at us like he was going to ram our trunk.

An eighteen-wheel truck sliced past in the outside lane, flashing its running lights as if thanking us for getting out of the way. I don't know how I missed seeing this truck coming. "We should just go," I said. "We should take the first exit."

"What if he takes it, too?" she said.

"I don't care. He's not quitting."

She checked her mirror, then looked over her right shoulder. "I'm getting back in the middle. I don't like this edge."

I checked the right side, a reflex as we moved right, and as I turned I heard his engine rev up, heard him come up on the inside again.

We were in the second lane and he was beside us, working the gun. Not at us, this time, but up in the air, pointing it straight up and wiggling it like he was showing it off to us. He shook it as if he wanted us to see only the gun, as if he was saying the gun is the thing, and then in a sudden sweeping move he brought the gun down and around and pushed the barrel hard up against his jaw and fired. There was a big explosion, light, firecracker sound, and blood sprayed out all over his face, his car tilted left, then back. Lily jerked toward me, then the other way, losing the steering wheel. The car shook, slipping sideways. The Camaro engine bucked and accelerated and the car came straight at us. I had my hands up by my head and got all the way down before I realized his car had slammed us, before I felt it. Then I didn't hear anything for a second, then metal scraping—we were sliding, the Camaro engine racing right at Lily's window, and she was slumped over. Our front end turned into the Camaro, toward it, and the Camaro slipped off us and shot behind us across the freeway. We jumped the curb, rammed head-on into the guardrail and started to spin; Lily flopped back against the seat, then forward and left against the driver's door, twisted down so her head slammed face forward into the door glass and the window frame. The glass was broken—had that happened before, or was it when she hit it? I didn't know. One of her wrists was tangled inside the steering wheel, her knee was up under it, too, on the door side, and we were scrubbing up and down on the median, riding the curb, but then the back end jumped the curb and hit the guardrail, crunching the driver's door into a steel pole, and that hit spun us the other direction, threw us out in the freeway backward until the front end went up the curb into the rail. We crashed hard, kicking the car up on the right wheels and slamming my door into a concrete piling. We hit again, bounced, skidded down the railing ripping off some fence, the right front wheel hooked on the guardrail and the back skip-hopping along the curb. That was it. We stopped when we hit the concrete base of a light standard.

. . .

Right then a truck went by going the other direction, separated from us by this concrete and this galvanized steel railing and the torn Cyclone fence. The truck carried two cabin cruisers, big ones, the boats roped onto the flatbed of this truck, tilted onto their sides so that from where I was you could see into the cabins, into the deck space.

All the way across the bottom level of this road concourse, across two complete highways, eight lanes each, and half of a third, maybe a hundred-fifty yards away, there was a white police car parked alongside the road behind a dune buggy that had a brilliant blue plastic tarp in place of a roof. The policeman had all the lights on his car turned on, the headlights and running lights and fog lights, the blinking taillights, the twirling lights in the center of the roof of his car and the flashing lights outboard of those, his driving lights, his turn signals. It even looked like the interior lights in this cop car were blinking.

I was trapped in the car, the door caved in and pinching my leg between it and the crumpled dash. I couldn't feel anything down there. But I was O.K. I looked at Lily. She wasn't as well off. We were facing backwards. Out her window I could see the Camaro, tipped up and into a concrete ditch on the other side of the freeway, and back from us. The rear end was still in the air.

I said, "Lily? Are you all right?" I punched at her with my left hand but her arm just slid forward. "Are you there? Jesus."

We were in a tunnel under two crossing freeways, one with a corkscrew exit that joined our lanes, and one that just passed over us. We were in a forest of evenly spaced columns, doubled sometimes, huge pillars ten feet in diameter, underneath three high roads probably fifty feet or more above us. I squinted up against the rain and all I saw were bottoms of freeways with strips of sky between them, dark blue, mottled, occasionally flashing. To my right, beyond the police car, there was that washboard incline up to grade level. Up there most of the buildings were old, two and three story, collapsing. There were a few lights up there, a few neon lights, bar signs, stuff that looked steamy and intriguing. Beyond that I saw the tops of the high-rises downtown, their stiffly patterned windows lit, their roofs decorated with more lights, their glass walls rippled mirrors of each other. I suddenly caught the pungent scent of gasoline and turned around in time to see a bright red GMC panel truck from the fifties rattle by, its exhaust peppering the concrete. This was a truck that was supposed to have doors on the side of it, but it didn't have any doors. The whole side was open and full of electronic gear neatly racked in metal shelving. The driver wasn't wearing a shirt.

From one of the overhead freeways came the howl of a tanker truck as it approached and then receded, going at some odd angle to us.

. . .

The cop tried to get straight across, but couldn't, so he trailed away up toward an exit. I sat there for a few more minutes until finally a kid in a red Jeep stopped to see what had happened. But he was terrified by what he saw so he left, and I listened—water outside, the whizzing of tires on the freeways above us, the odd clank of metal against metal, like a pulley on a flagpole, that I only heard when there were no cars, the rush of the wind blowing across that wet concrete, rattling the loose chain-link fence, the click of the car's turn signal that was stuck on when we hit—I was going in and out. Then the sound of voices, people out of their cars but too far away for me to hear what they were saying, the occasional high-pitched horn of a driver. I stared at the high pole ahead of me, at the haloed amber bulb in its box, discreet anodized-aluminum box, architectural, very correct, stared at the odd light that seemed to evaporate darkness, dry it up into a flat, inarticulate, colorless light that just barely rested on what it lit.

I wanted some magic, something else. I was there a foot from Lily and she was twisted up and there was some blood and I knew she wasn't going to make it, maybe hadn't made it. I imagined holding her the way people hold people in movies, but I couldn't because of the dashboard and the door broken off its hinges and driven sideways into the foot well, wedging me in. Her door had collapsed inward at the center. The glass was out of the windshield and the pole that holds the roof was crushed, broken, hanging loose in front of her. I thought of pulling her back off the steering wheel, which I saw now was cracked, one of the spokes gone, but decided I couldn't. So I only looked, reached my left hand and pressed three or four fingers on her forearm, stroked down into the open palm of her right hand, the forearm and hand bent backward at the elbow so that they lay along the front edge of the seat. The arm was broken, twisted unnaturally.

Then somebody had red hazard lights on the road behind us, flarelike lights, burning with the intensity of fireworks, but stationary, the starry flutter of the light crimson, graduated from center to edge, very intense, like lipstick dizzyingly caught in match light. I noticed the nail on Lily's third finger was cut but still hanging on. I shouldn't touch her, I kept saying to myself. Don't touch her. You can't do anything. Maybe they can.

I did not hear the siren until the emergency truck was right beside us, and then it blasted into my head, its wail an unthinkable disorientation; it felt as if the sound was moving things by itself, as if the car was rocking against the galvanized rail and the huge lamp pole that was steady out over the road. Two guys, three guys were there at Lily's door. They got it off fast. It wasn't hard. Then they were grabbing at her, one guy already ripping away her shirt, checking her neck, smearing the blood there aside so he could see what he was touching, the third guy was sent back to the truck for something. More people outside the car, some on her side, fewer on mine, all in big black slick coats with yellow collars, guys in boots yelling *Was I O.K.?* and me yelling back that I was, or thinking I was yelling back that I was, hearing myself yell back, but they kept asking anyway, I didn't know why.

There was an empty beer bottle, a Czech beer I'd bought because the label was snazzy, on the floor of the car. The bottle rolled as the guys at Lily's door worked to get her out. One of them looked at me staring and he said, "Are you all right? Can you hear me?"

I think I nodded. I think I said "Yes" to both questions.

Behind this guy, who was trying to free Lily's seat belt and had resorted to cutting it with garden shears somebody had handed over his shoulder, there was a man who had a radio transmitter, hand held, that made a lot of noise. He was talking into this thing, then listening to it. It was like TV. I sat in the passenger seat and watched it all unfold. Nothing surprised or startled me, nothing worried me. I knew what he was saying, had known it since the astonishing electric crack of the pistol and the way we hit the first time, the way Lily had moved like a dummy, like stuffed clothes. The rest was slow motion, the feeling of weightlessness when the car twisted and jacked up and then everything delicate at once, hitting, screeching off the guardrail and the chain-link fence above it into the steel light pole, pulling yards of ripped-out fence along, the sounds of metal stretching.

The guys in their big coats had stepped back for a conference outside and slightly back of the door opening, so I saw only legs, three pairs and one stray, all jeans. I couldn't get the conversation, though I saw a hand slide back into my line of sight, a pointing finger.

I thought of Charles and everything froze. My skin seemed like it was shaking. Where would he see her first? I couldn't imagine that for him. Or what it was going to be like. His brain was too small, too uncluttered, I couldn't get there. I couldn't feel the way he would feel, I couldn't think ahead of him so I would always be ready. I couldn't protect him.

Suddenly I didn't want these guys seeing her, I didn't want anyone seeing her, I didn't like what anybody did, what they were doing. Caged up there in the car more than anything I wanted a chance to see Lily in the hospital, to see her name on that slotted metal rectangle outside the door, to see OXYGEN in Magic Marker on a thick piece of masking tape, torn off at both ends and smoothed onto the panel, to see her there on a chrome bed with its thin mattress, turned onto her side, her knees drawn up, her hands at her mouth.

I wanted to worry about the hall light hitting her eyes, disturbing her, about it creasing the room and the walls, slicing diagonally across ceiling and floor, across her bed when I opened the door, to worry that the door might be too heavy for her when she was ready to start getting up, to start walking in the halls, to worry about disturbing her on my late-night visits, slipping through the light from the opened door, sidestepping the table with her tray still on it, checking what she'd eaten and what she'd left on the tray, to worry as I stood by the bed and touched her damp face that she looked waxy, a likeness of herself, a candid shot blown actual size.

She would draw a hand across her mouth and groan, turning. The room would be dark and quiet except for the numbers on her IV stand, the numbers on her heart and oxygen monitors, the clicking numbers, the quiet pumps, the sounds of small liquids shuttling through tubes. I'd go past the bed to the window, look out at the clear night after the impenetrable overcast of the day, at the high clouds, bright, protecting a whitish moon that looked as if it would always be there, generous, idle, comforting. Then I would look down at the street below, the hospital lot, I would try to find my car there, then watch the tops of other cars, people getting in and out, then drop the curtain and notice pale light from the street snake in around the edges of the fabric, glowing.

I would sit for hours in the hospital armchair in the corner of her room and rub my eyes, which would burn, and I would wait for her in that room, I would see us there, looking like nothing special, like people with a future amid the equipment lights that blinked then played rock-steady, shining, clicking, flicking forward a few digits, backward a few, green numbers on black backgrounds on blue machines, green lines on beige ceiling-mounted monitors, all those steady numbers, glassy plastic tubes sliding under sheets, joined and rejoined, clipped here and there with blue box clips, tape on her wrists, bruises, and above her, hooked on the chrome stand, collapsing sacks of clear liquids, one opaque sack, brown plastic, the color of a certain leaf bag we often bought at the grocery. I wanted that chance. I wanted her. I would have given anything.

Printed in the United States
by Baker & Taylor Publisher Services